THE GOSPEL MIRROR

AND OTHER SERMONS

THE GOSPEL MIRROR

AND OTHER SERMONS

By

WILLIAM RILEY BENHAM, A.M., D.D.

Edited by

Rev. ANDREW GILLIES
St. Andrew's Church, New York

NEW YORK
MCMIII

WILDSIDE PRESS

WILLIAM RILEY BENHAM, A.M., D.D.

IN GRATEFUL MEMORY OF

A LOVING HEART · A GREAT SOUL

A NOBLE LIFE

PREFACE

THIS little volume is not sent out as representative of the best work of him whose name it bears. His noblest utterances are beyond type and press. In the purest form of extemporaneous preaching they fell hot from his anointed lips to attain immortality only in the hearts and characters of those who heard them. The manuscripts which he left behind were but fragments and frameworks, sacred remnants of a faithful servant's work. But William Riley Benham had endeared himself to a great and widely scattered throng. "He was a choice spirit. His was a life beautiful." As principal of Genesee Wesleyan Seminary he won to himself the hundreds of students and exalted before them the glory of the Christ life. As pastor of a dozen churches in the Genesee and Central New York conferences he builded mightily for the kingdom of God. As a humble servant of his Lord and Christ, tender, tactful, patient, self-sacrificing, he became as a light set on a hill. So it is not strange that a multitude have expressed the desire for a memorial of him whom they knew and loved. It is in answer to that spontaneous request that these sermons have been selected and published. Imperfect they must be, as voices of him who preached them; but, by the power of that Spirit which beautified his life, may they help to perpetuate his blessed influence and fulfil the Divine declaration, "He, being dead, yet speaketh."

CONTENTS

I

THE GOSPEL MIRROR

" But we all, with open face beholding as in a glass the glory of the Lord, are changed into the same image from glory to glory, even as by the Spirit of the Lord."

II. CORINTHIANS iii. 18.

EVERY religious change begins in thought. Indeed, it is not yet proved but that all change begins in thought. Every new development in Christian character germinates and unfolds in thought, and even though the agent be the Spirit of God, still He respects the sovereignty of our nature, working within us to will and to do according to the laws of mind. It is difficult to make even good men always feel the necessity of right thinking and the force of the fact, "As a man thinketh in his heart so is he."

But the operation of the law is not confined to the regenerate. To every man there appears a vision. Joined to the consciousness of what we are is the conception and conviction of what we ought to be: that ever-present standard of reference and comparison; that inspiring something for which the good man pants; that which often pursues the guilty soul like an avenging spirit, to which an accusing conscience ever points in her fiery argument; that sad "might have been," which, by its very contrast, makes the awakened sinner almost despair. And there is a mysterious process by which these floating images of thought are interwoven into the very fibre of our being, so that for infinite reasons we must be careful not only that we think right and that we cherish the truth, but also that it be a divine ideal which is shining in the soul, a divine ideal of life and character.

We all know from whence we derive our ideas of perfection in the intellectual world. We combine the dim remembrance of the grand and beautiful in word and art that we have seen and heard with the original in our own minds. The mountain, the forest, the stream, the sky, all enter into our vision of perfection, as the artist unconsciously gets a feature here, an expression there, which helps form the living design of his thought to be transferred to the living canvas. So that our keenness of perception, our sense of sublimity, and the scenery from which we draw must coin our conception of the beautiful. Thus without the gospel must we coin our idea of the right and good, and so we must find the great Personality of God. We must glean from nature what we can of God's image, listen to the winds and waves for His voice, and combine these lisping consonants of truth with the law written in our hearts. But there is a veil on that law, and how dark and hideous, like some graven image of the world's idolatry, would be our idea of God thus revealed, for

we cannot now read all that is meant in nature. We
can pick the flowers to pieces and tell the genus and
class to which they belong; we can break open a stone
and guess of what it is made, what plants and beings
are sepulchred in it, and sometimes how old it is; we
can catch a sunbeam or a star-ray and by our glass tell
what is on fire in the distant orb; and we know that all
this is the incarnation of wonderful thought and beauty,
and that a force is under and in it which is next to almighty; but this is not much of God. We do not feel
the heart which is beating through the world; we do
not know the soul which is burning beyond the stars.
There may, there must, be more of God revealed in
nature than we see; more of His glory in the heavens;
more of His voice than we hear in the speech that day
unto day uttereth; perhaps there is a theodicy in this
other Bible which would declare Him and a hand might
touch our eyes until they see like Stephen's; but there
is a veil on our hearts as on the mind of Israel before
the law, a veil over the green earth and the bright
heavens and over every chapter of His providence.

We may go out by day or by night and drink in
mighty thoughts of Him who holds up the unpillared
universe; we may go amid some grand mountain scenery and feel our hearts swell at the greatness which
lifted these massive monuments upon their rocky base
and at the majesty which reigns in that wild solitude,

but they are only thoughts of His genius, thoughts of His power.

We might have been among the throng which stood before the old Mount in the desert and seen it smoke and flame and rock with the thunder as Moses went up to the cloudy pavilion of Jehovah. We might have seen that original engraving of God upon the stony tablets and that majestic code, that higher law, that transcript of the eternal Mind. There was something of God's glory; there was grandeur, but it was a terrible majesty; it was a fearful glory that shone from the summit of Sinai; a ministration of death crowned with a lightning wreath flashing in every face, "Our God is a consuming fire."

No, we have not come to the bleak hills and empty caves of nature; we have not come to the Mount which might be touched, but we have come unto Mount Zion. There we stand beneath that blood and see the real Shekinah, the glory of the Lord, in the face of Jesus Christ; there it is written in crimson glory: "God is love." "For God, who commanded the light to shine out of darkness, hath shined in our hearts, to give the light of the knowledge of the glory of God in the face of Jesus Christ." And we, beholding that glory in Jesus, His life, His character, His love, reflected in that fiery light of the Spirit from the great burnished mirror of the Gospel, are changed from glory to glory.

THE GOSPEL MIRROR

Here is the divine statement of the great law of moral assimilation. We often· speak of the influence we exert. Here at least we are original; we create this fearful power; but we are just as susceptible to influence; we receive as well as create. It is as true of the body as it is of the plant that it is affected by climate, seasons, food. What instincts are planted in us to shield us from accident and malaria! And yet how much more sensitive is the soul. It has so many points of contact; through every sense it stretches out and touches the world; its eyes are open to every scene; its listening ears catch every sound; its tender feet feel every thorn in its path; its trembling lungs inhale an atmosphere charged with moral pestilence, or they breathe the aroma of the skies; and, on its mighty wings of thought and fancy, we can outstrip the halting sense and roam the universe like a spirit.

But while any passing scene may leave its image on the mind; while even an impure breath may touch and taint us without volition, it is not true that our strongest moral or mental traits, our characters, are transformed in this general passive way. The soul must, in some degree, be enlisted into the service of the transforming object. Thus men become like their professions in life. Let one devote himself exclusively to an art or science and his mind will develop, by the law of habit, a peculiar aptness or trait for that work. If there is an original talent it will unfold, and, too, the work often will create the talent. So the mathematician is filled with figures and formulas; wherever he goes the process continues and he measures angles and distances among the flowers and streams, and upon the bright heavens sees only great curves and lines and magnitudes, sines and cosines. The artist sees only pictures, the geologist specimens, and, to the mechanic, the world becomes a great machine, not merely because the mind works in the line of interest or duty, but because it acts automatically. It springs to the pursuit of its elect idea like a hound on the chase, keen and happy in its toil. Thus the hand of the musician gets cunning and the soul becomes keyed to exquisite harmonies. Thus great spirits like Columbus and Bacon and Kepler have become sharp-sighted to see things out of sight, worlds beyond the waters, and continents in the air. Thus in any sphere of life a master aim transforms the mental being and begets a master genius. It is by beholding, enchaining the thought, the eye, upon an object, until it becomes vivid and its methods and colors flow into and play around the soul in their strange delicate tuition. So it is by holding the attention, beholding as in a glass this glory of the Lord, until its inherent beauty, its peculiar features, its divine methods, its holy ministry are indelibly vivid in the thought.

6

THE GOSPEL MIRROR

The moral nature is just as susceptible as the intellectual. It may take more to create an artistic taste, a scientific mind, than to fashion our souls after the model we ordain, and yet it is by beholding. One may accustom himself to look upon the false or obscene, whether in books, statuary, or painting, and he will soon become base as the object he contemplates; we can transform ourselves into demons by dwelling upon the devilish, or we may become angelic by looking at the heavenly. And there are some things which may appear pure and innocent but are thus proven to be deadly. We cannot tear off the mask of the white devil, but we can lift the veil of the heart where he has been and see the black blight of his breath upon the delicate beauty of the spirit. "By their fruits ye shall know them."

Whether an idea or practice, the image must produce after its kind. If evil, it will excite its own evil thought and passions, which will lust against conscience, against reason, and bribe the will, and then its dim features will begin to appear, like its shadow, in the soul; another look, another indulgence and another, until its shape of sin stands out in all the ugliness of its dark original. The longer he gazes on the alluring thing the more radically is he changed, until he becomes its living incarnation, staggering in the delirium of his sin down his crooked path to hell. We are often startled at the sudden fall of one we had thought a paragon of morality, but the history of that heart would reveal the mystery. He began the new departure in thought; he was first seduced in thought; he crucified Christ within before he held Him up to open shame. One does not go from prayer to blasphemy, from the closet to the brothel, from love to murder, from the summit to the abyss at a leap. The logic of Satan is too subtle to place the assassin's tools in the hand of love, or show the drunkard's grave in the first glass, or disclose to the eyes of purity the hell of infamy. There intervenes this process of education: the devil depraves the imagination, enthrones himself there in some specious sin, some charming shape, ever changing as he works out his mission, until he lays aside his last angelic feature, the last remnant of his white robe, and confronts his own image in a human soul.

We see another example of this law in this fact. Looking upon men or their written lives, we associate the greatness of their intellect or genius with their moral character, and, if that be vicious, our hatred of vice is lessened as we admire their power. Bold, bald, brazen, stupid wickedness shocks and disgusts men; hence it seldom appears in its serpentine form; evil is mixed with good, the hellish with the heroic. Some authors so paint their hero that though he may be the veriest wretch that ever escaped the halter, we are compelled to sympathize with him; they will so bleach out his crime, gild and varnish his spotted soul with some generous trait or brilliancy that we cannot help admiring. Byron had the power of investing the most contemptible character that a totally depraved imagination could create with qualities that almost make us forget the bad. Milton's devil is one of the grandest characters of all literature, divested of that meanness and slime of the snake nature, nearly as unlike the real old serpent as when he stood clothed in light at the court of heaven. So by associating greatness with any sin we come almost to tolerate, if not admire, the sin; thus the hero of a criminal tale is often realized in the person of the reader; he aspires to be the adroit, brilliant villain, but becomes only the villain. This genius of sin is very cheap, it does not take much talent. Anyone can be wicked.

So, by feeding upon characters which blend goodness with greatness, biographies of splendid virtue, illustrious purity and talent, do we become good and great. And beholding in this gospel mirror a glory, a person, in whom all that is beautiful, all that is manly and divine, all that is immaculate and lovely, wedded to all that is great in the Godhead, must we not be transformed as we gaze? Must it not stir our aspirations and start our prayers? Are we so bad that we cannot feel the holy fascination? Is there not glory enough in Jesus to repeat itself in the human soul?

THE GOSPEL MIRROR

This sort of transformation, however, supposes a previous change, a preparation. The apostle makes just this invidious distinction. "We, apostles, Christians, beholding." Here, as in all the gospel and in every gospel sermon, comes in the cross; here we see the blood; here is the offence. "Ye must be born of the Spirit." A wicked man with all his sinful antipathies and selfishness cannot change his character by this natural process; change his hating, hideous nature into the image of purity and love by merely looking at the pure and lovely Christ, any more than by thought and volition he can transform his ugly body into the beauty of the sculptor's chiselled statue. If he can look himself into tears it is well, for he must be melted before he can be moulded by even a divine hand; but he must also be born of the Spirit. Take the plate of the old daguerreotype before it is prepared by the chemical process, put it in the camera and tell the sunbeams to come in the aperture and imprint the likeness, but they might shine and shine forever with all their unclouded splendor and not make an impression. So might this glory of the Lord in the gospel in all its celestial brightness shine upon the sinner's hard heart without creating the image of God until it has been prepared by the renewing of the Holy Ghost. No, the plate in the instrument must be made sensitive to the light by the action of chemicals and the heavy black veil lifted from the eye of the

camera, and then God's artist will come flashing in to
paint the likeness on that retina. When the hard dark
nature feels this process of grace, its stains of sin washed
out in blood and made sensitive to holiness; when the
black veil which shrouds the truth is lifted, then the glory
of the Lord will flood the soul and the transfiguring power of Christ's intrinsic beauty be felt as never before,
changing us from glory to glory.

Then, not only are we made free by the Spirit to see
this glory, for that is the meaning of "where the Spirit
of the Lord is there is liberty"; but now Jesus is en-
throned as the ideal of our love. Do you know what
that means? There is one who has set up on the throne
of his affections wealth; let that be his ideal, that his
golden god which he worships and to which he renders
up his daily account in dollars and cents, and how long
before every generous emotion is gone, every love
curdled, conscience coined, hope of glory pawned? How
long before that image is realized in his depraved miser's
soul? It is not that money is evil, but the love of it;
it is good as a medium of exchange, but will not do for
a god. Let it be sensuality, any form of vice, which is
enshrined in the heart and how soon the angel flies;
then how fast the demon grows, until the blush of beauty
perishes, and the spotted ghastly face of lust is in the
soul; the brand of the beast is on the forehead. Let it be
any dear ambition and how controlling, how transform-

ing; it is the power of love which aspires and imitates and catches the spirit of its idol whether that idol is an idea or a man. It is this which made the Old Guard of Napoleon invincible, which made one of them say, as the physician in probing for a bullet cut near the heart, "Probe a little deeper and you will find the Emperor."

As Christ is now the ideal of our love, as He is our moral hero, how glorious He seems to us, how divine all His acts and words as we follow Him again over Judæa to the cross; how charming every trait of His character, how ineffable His purity, how transcendent His love; how beautiful to us our "Rose of Sharon." His glory is more glorious in our eyes the more we love, and so we drink in His spirit, we look for His footsteps, we long and pray to be like Jesus. So this master passion beholding this glory changes us from glory to glory. Our love beholding glorifies Christ and the glory of Christ transfigures us.

Again, this beholding transforms because of its insulating power, warding off evil. Men say often that we are the creatures of circumstances. There are influences which crowd the world and strike us on every side, to sway and mould and create us. They may do harm to passive dead souls which float on the tide; but we have the antidote: it is beholding, it is the prepossession of Christ. We all know what it is to have an idea, an aim, a great joy or grief so burning in the soul that we can go through jostling crowds and noise and bustle unconscious of all but the one thing.

So the siren may sing, subtle forces throng us, fiery darts be thick in the air, the glory of the world flash, the magnetic currents of hell whirl around us, the shafts of envy and the breath of devils fly in our faces, but by this holy insulation we may be intact, by the divine sovereignty of mind holding the eye upon that glory of Christ until it charms, fascinates, and dominates the soul. The old world rolls on unheeded and the blasts of hell sweep by unfelt. Like Bunyan's Pilgrim, our fingers in our ears and our eyes on the glory, we run crying, "Life, eternal life."

Beholding! Yes, this glory may become the great idea; greater than the thought of the unchaste, greater than the love of gold, or any other passion; the sun of man's life about which he revolves in his orbit of duty, with its glory in his eye and in the soul, every ray pregnant with its transforming life, until he becomes transparent and glowing and sunlike, glory to glory.

It is the one idea, Christ first, constant, pre-eminent. It is the diverted gaze which makes the blurred picture. When you sit for a photograph the more steady the eye, the more perfect the isolation, the clearer the image. So by looking at Jesus the spell of the world is broken and none of the power of His glory is lost until He sees

His own face in us, true as the Spirit and beautiful as holiness. It is said that Luther had but one idea and that was Jesus.

We see, then, that there is a strange power in our ideal. It is not always the man who works the hardest who succeeds the best, but the man who thinks the hardest and best. This thought-life is not mere poetry; it is the unwritten history of every life; it is the matter which makes character. This floating form which we cherish as our goal casts its shadow over the soul and is the prototype of what we shall be. These light fancies may be crystallized into immortality. It is said that the sailor whose home is on the deep, living in the midst of storms, beholding old ocean in its strange moods, catches something of its wild restless spirit and is a proverb of everything that is open and generous; that the Italian, wrapped in the luxurious beauty of his home, looking into a sky of heavenly depth and into night's arch blazing with matchless glories, in his mental being inherits something of that grace and fiery temper; that the Swiss, in his mountain home, revelling amid the rugged scenery of his grand Alps, drinks in something of their sublimity; but we inherit most from the scenery of the spiritual world where we live, and it may be like that which is swarming the haunts of vice or which floated around the rocky home of the old apostle—our world may be a brothel or a Patmos.

THE GOSPEL MIRROR

Now all of us elect an ideal in every sphere of work and it becomes a real part of us. It is not an ethereal cloud painted by a sunbeam, torn and tossed by every fitful breeze; it is not a mocking image now appearing and then vanishing, but to us a bright angel form ever hovering over us. God put it there in our natures, firing our souls to imitate her beauty, and though we do not hope to embody all her features of loveliness, yet ever gazing upon them we feel the ministry of her inspiring presence. This ideal is the orator's unspoken eloquence, the poet's unwritten poesy; it was the painting of Raphael before his hand touched the canvas; the breathing statues of Angelo before his chisel fashioned the marble; it was the Iliad when it was burning in the soul of the blind wanderer of Greece; it was this beautiful world when it was slumbering in the mind of the Infinite; it was this quiet land of civil and religious freedom when our fathers stood on Plymouth Rock; it was this glorious fabric of independent union when it inspired the heroic hearts of '76, when they struck the first glad note of liberty, when with desperate valor for seven long years they were building it with blood; it was the chaos of sin, of death, and tears, when it floated a foul vision in the black soul of the prince of devils; and it was the new paradise which shone in the eye of Christ, when He was with the Father, through the mists of death and the shadows of Calvary, and

15

which brought Him from the skies. And that love, that character, is the real glory, the transcendent ideal, we are beholding, and it is the glory this world is beholding which is changing it into the likeness of heaven.

We need not fear because it is so glorious. We must have a high, a perfect ideal for our chosen life, for, however low it is, we never transcend. If we believe we must carry to the last gasp some sin, wear some mark of the beast, some resemblance to Satan, we shall not be delivered from this body of death; the life never transcends its ideal. The savage who has no higher idea of happiness than his own wild life, no better morality than love for his friend and a tomahawk for his foe, never outgrows that life; the heathen who had no purer god than Jupiter, no higher heaven than Olympus, in his character embodied the carnal attributes of his mystic deity and was scarcely fit for his own sensual Elysium of the gods.

Why does the artist study a masterpiece instead of a daub? What if it does shame his best efforts now, it will stir his genius. And if we should attain this character in all its glory, we need not fear becoming divine or losing our identity, as some have talked. All photographs of the sun are but a dark blot, an outline, and this image is but a faint picture of God and not God. This room full of light is not all light, much less the great burning reservoir in the heavens. As the budding lily looks into the face of the sun and opens its snowy petals at his charms, in its whiteness it is a perfect image of the sun, and yet it is only a lily; a crystal drop is big enough to hold a miniature spectrum of the sun like that which is bent on the sky and yet it may be only a tear; it is only a ray of His glory entering and filling our little apartment with its radiance, and though we come to mirror again the glory we see in the gospel, be it ever so perfect, it is only a lily, only a tear in its transfiguration. No, it is not to become gods in wisdom, but godlike in love. "O, to be like God in this." It is the greatest prayer ever made; it is the highest wish of angels; it is the best heritage of the universe. It is the grandest metamorphosis in all the creation of God, from glory to glory.

Let us not put up our notion, our ism, our dark foolish design, let us take Christ, His glory; not Plato's ideal man or any other man's ideal, but Christ, "looking unto Jesus." Let us not set up self, this great "I" for our model or for our thought, for then we shall become more like ourselves and we want less of self and more of Christ, less of our nature and more of the divine nature; and often the more we look at ourselves and our defects, even for religious analysis, the more we become morbid and doubting and despairing.

Let us look away to this glory even for our outward life and inspiration in doing good. This is our ideal, the Lord's Christ, to walk as He walked, work as He worked, to sacrifice like Jesus. I have somewhere read of an old artist who had begun the masterpiece of his life; he had but partially completed it when his hand was unstrung by fatal illness; he called his student to his bedside and told him his plans and commanded him to finish the work. The student pleaded his incompetency, but to every excuse the answer was "Do thy best." He went to the studio, and as he looked upon the painting, he caught the idea and his soul, inspiration, the fire of slumbering genius was aroused, he took the brush, his hand grew steady, and, with his glowing eye on the model he painted until it was done; it was a triumph of art, and the applause of the master was his.

So we may tremble and stand in awe of our great work of life, for we paint for immortality; but we have a pattern; not an outline, but a finished masterpiece; and we may work from this model, catching its divine thought, feeling its unearthly beauty, and, with a holier inspiration than genius, show something of the Master's glory, even as our souls are transfigured, beholding His image, from glory to glory.

II

FIGS OR THISTLES

"For none of us liveth to himself."

ROMANS xiv. 7.

WHILE this is the law of the Christian, the spring and moving force of whose life is Christ, it is also true in an absolute sense. The first thing we have to learn is that we are not our own, and it is a hard thing to learn. Selfishness is the great generic vice of our nature; it is born in us, and, as one has said, "thrives very well without any means of grace."

The tuition against it begins in the cradle. The mother takes the babe in her arms, looks into his laughing eyes, and says, "You are mine"; she sings it in every lullaby and breathes it in every caress. But often, in spite of her songs and tenderness, this perverse spirit grows into a rebel which will not be conquered even by a mother's heart. It may melt a little at her tears, and bleed and bend beneath the chastening rod, but it lives and thrives and creeps forth in all the protean forms of sin. In all the plans of life, in the ambitions, the castle-building, is seen the black hand of this artist. Even in the romance of youth, the bright visions and hopes which gather around these early

19

years, this evil genius must often be the inspiration, and always the hero. In every scene of beauty, in every holy place, in every grand endeavor, this great "I" must be the ideal forever.

Again, ere one steps from the shelter of home, ere he passes from parental authority, the State puts its hand upon him and says, "You are not your own"; and hands that are thrust out from every side of the living world hold him for service.

Upon his soul is felt, too, the pressure of a claim higher than all, and in the very sanctuary of his being echoes a voice, "You are not your own." That consciousness of divine ownership is the first factor in salvation; it is the basis of conviction. If he is his own he may do what he will with his own. He is not only a law unto himself, but a judge; he need bend at no other altar; he need crown no other Lord; he is his own sovereign. But he sees the brand of a supreme ownership upon his brow, upon every power of his spirit, and every limb of his body, pencilled by the sunlight throughout the great Kosmos, upon the wings of the insect, and the bosom of the worlds, "ever singing as they shine, the hand that made us is divine." It is God's universe. Man has not a clear title to an atom. He does not own a heart-beat. And still he may ignore God's right in him, and, like Napoleon, put the crown upon his own head, an ominous sign of his ultimate dethronement.

And above all, we have seen those whose feet have just touched the threshold of life, upon them the crisis of destiny, turn away from the altar of God, over which is written in blood, "Ye are not your own," to immolate themselves upon the shrine of their own lusts.

Against this desperate tide of our nature God sets up the barriers of home, society, and conscience; against it He protests by all the blessed ministries of love, by all the might of duty. Against it He legislates. It burns in every edict of Sinai, in every syllable of nature, and is the end of every commandment. Against it He holds up the cross; in this crimson sign against our little selfish hearts, He puts His great heart of mercy and love, with every throb saying, "Ye are not your own." ·

Yet men may resist Him and say, "Who is the Lord that we should serve Him?" Yes, we may have our own way, hurl ourselves against omnipotence and be crushed; we may wreck ourselves upon our own passions and go down. Even then it will be true: "None of us liveth to himself, and no man dieth unto himself." It is not possible; Judas did not live unto himself any more than Jesus. We have no choice here. We must live, and we cannot stop the outgoings of that life. We may say what it shall be, a blight or a blessing, but God has started a force in us which will go out from us and smite human hearts for good or ill, and it will go on and touch other destinies forever.

THE GOSPEL MIRROR

This comes from the necessary relations in which God has bound us up together, in social and business and State and national dependencies. There mind touches mind, hand touches hand, heart beats against heart, from house to house, from village to village, from city to city, along thoroughfares, over mountains, across seas, around the world, and over the gulf of space from world to world, up the golden staircase to the throne. "God hath made of one blood all the nations of the earth," and God is the father of the world. The race is one great body, and we are members one of another, embraced by one atmosphere, chained together by a gravity which no man can put asunder. And because we are put in this mysterious realm of being as into a vast sea of life quivering with immortal issues, we possess this fearful power. We cannot stir an oar but that the circling waves go out and on until they throb and break on an eternal shore. As I have said, we cannot stop the outflowing of this life in us. It is an original spring and we cannot dam up its streams and roll them back upon themselves. They will rise higher and burst out somewhere like the jets of an artificial fountain. You cannot cramp the mind with the vice of the will and hold it fast, nor fold the wings of fancy, nor chain the fiery steeds of passion forever. There are no fetters forged in earth or heaven which can bind the immortal spirit unless its links are made of love. Like Sampson, it will burst them asunder. It will think and dream and aspire and send out its thoughts, its volitions, its loves and hates into the world. Whether in speech or song or action, somehow it will come out; it will reveal itself in some creation; it is irrepressible; it is the necessity of all life to unfold itself.

As well try by some magic to thrust back the beauty and odor of the flower into its bosom, and push in the buds of the tree; as well try to muzzle the birds, and throttle the winds, or roll back the sunlight to its source, as to repress the outgoings of your soul. You may seal up one avenue and they will leap to another. Put out the eye and palsy the tongue, and it will creep out from the fingers and find a tongue for its songs and words to lisp its visions; rob it of every medium and it will burst its clay dungeon and fly away.

What else could a man do with some great purpose or invention—an Ericsson with a Monitor, a Homer with an Iliad, or a Newton with his *Principia*—in his brain with no outlet? What else could he do but die? How could the old prophet live with the word of the Lord shut up in his soul, or John with the revelations of Patmos, or a man full of the riches of grace and unspeakable joy, if he could not speak it forth? The life of sin, too, is just as irrepressible, and will appear through all disguises in its own nature. These are too thin and transient to conceal its amities. You cannot filter the poison of a corrupt heart through the forms of religion, the outward service of any church, and send it out the pure sweet stream of love. Men do not gather grapes from thorns or figs from thistles. Nature will out. If there is melody in the man he will sing, with music or without it. If the visions of an artist are glowing in his soul, those features of beauty will appear on the canvas; or, if the dark genius of sin abides within, its hideous dream will be felt if it does not appear in bold relief; the leaf and the petal will advertise the germ. The liquid notes which float to our ears bring the name of the songster. You cannot teach the lark's song to the raven. There is no art by which we may hide or transform our real nature as it flows out from the fountain.

If a tree is evil we may graft upon every limb some noble stock, and for its sake they may bear some good fruit, but beneath it all the old trunk will thrust out some twig or leaf to let out its original nature. So one may have an evil, selfish heart and engraft his hands with the deeds of charity, and his lips with the speech of angels, but the bitter sap within will creep forth in common unconscious life and betray him, and he will, after all, cast the shadow of the Upas. Oh, that we might feel this! In spite of our most earnest, honest efforts to mould this moral force which goes out from us, we exhale our real life from every pore. The genius of our nature stands out of us by our side, our true shadow as we move among men. And wherever it falls it will be like the shadow of Peter into which they brought the sick for healing, or like a deep blighting eclipse.

We cannot prevent the power of our life upon others; the heart has no rod to carry off its fires like that which takes the wrath from the clouds. If all the evil which flows out from us could only strike against other minds and hearts like waves against a rock, leaving no mark, it would not be so fearful, though they rebound and drown us in shame and sorrow. If only these voices we have spoken into the air could all come back to us like echoes, having entered no soul, it would not be so sad though they reverberate forever in memory. Alas, for the truth, they come back not only for retribution, but mingled with wails of souls they have smitten.

How sensitive people are to this power. We drink it in as the world does the sunshine. It mingles with our thoughts, flows in upon the sensibilities, mars the will, and is crystallized in character. It comes stealthily; it utters no voice, sounds no trumpet, flies no signal, and glides into our hearts like a spirit. It often enters, as ours goes out, unconsciously; we may feel no shock, no thrill, no swaying of the emotions as by a tempest, no strain upon the will, no soul shrinking, and yet, subtle as ether, it may infuse itself throughout our being and tinge and turn the current of our life by its influence.

25

THE GOSPEL MIRROR

We walk amid some picturesque scenery and the rugged rocks, the wild torrents, the crystal fountains, picture themselves in the eye, and mysteriously upon the mind. We did not feel the changes, and yet we may carry them forever. We walk the street, mingle in society, attend the theatre, and the faces and words of men, the scenes enacted, are drawn by a limner upon the soul in fast colors; yet the sensitive canvas did not feel the brush of the artist. One may walk through places where he knows there is peril, unconscious of evil, and yet upon the delicate beauty of the soul is the blight of death; holy hope and virtue, like the blush of flowers, are withered as if he had passed the mouth of the pit and felt the breath of devils.

In the far Southwest is a valley to enter which is death. In its bottom are gurgling crystal springs, but they generate carbonic acid gas, and not a bush or green thing is seen there, not a flower or blade of grass. Beside these springs are bleaching the bones of animals and ghastly skeletons of men. Upon an eminence near is a pillar, planted by some benevolent hand, engraved the "Valley of Death. Enter not." There are many such places in the world, where sparkling fountains rise and gurgle like the siren's song, to allure the thirsty seekers of pleasure. Around them are the wrecks of human souls, the ghastly *débris* of precious lives and intellects, every green thing blighted by the corroding air, and a

sentinel at every gate.   Yet the way is made smooth
by the feet of the thoughtless crowd going down to
the valley of the shadow of death.

Against much of this subtle power we cannot insulate
ourselves. It floods us; we cannot wholly help the force
of the ideas, the actions, the fashions, the opinions, the
characters of men among whom we live. I cannot stand
here to-night and have the same thoughts and feelings
as if I were here alone; your looks affect me; your
faces, opinions, sympathies, and presence enter into me;
they strangely affect this heart of mine. I cannot
help it.

You cannot walk the street and feel and act as you
would if alone. Our lives intermingle more than we
dream, and by no artificial exclusiveness can we shield
ourselves from the power of the lowest life around us.
Men have buried themselves in monasteries to preserve
their sanctity and to keep off the world, but the whole
sad history of asceticism shows it was a failure. There
was human nature within. This great world battery will
go upon the wings of thought and memory, and this
subtle electricity would flow through solid blocks of
stone; as well try to keep the oxygen out of the blood
as this all-embracing life of society out of the soul. The
world touches us on every side and soaks into us. So,
while we would not dishonor the germ in its power of
assimilation, the man in us which makes us responsible,

we cannot utterly insulate ourselves from the power of human hearts which crowd against us.

Sometimes we see a man, some scholar in whom seems concentrated all the culture of the past; in his brain appear to exist all the thought and history of the world. So to some extent in every man we may behold the culmination of all the influences of his circle for the ages. If he passively drinks them in with no shield of faith, no breastplate of righteousness, no counter energy, he may become but the incarnation of these forces (and the world is crowded with such men), a thing of chance, drifting on the last tide which strikes him.

This atmosphere so well illustrates it. It is the medium of light. Without it, though the king of day still rode in his course, we should be in a frigid zone of darkness. So this strange human influence and sympathy are often the medium of God's sunshine. How much of His grace comes through human hands and hearts, as all His grace and glory flow through the suffering life and broken heart of Jesus. This power is the medium, too, by which men are possessed with demons. It is a human hand and not that of a fiend which presses the cup of woe and blood to the lips of a brother. This social power is the mighty arm which gathers in the young to the marble altar; it is the siren which charms them to the chambers of hell; it is the genius of devils. The air may come in gentle breezes, with life and sympathy, freighted with sweet odors; it may come in cold wrecking storms, and in the simooms on the desert; there are currents in the upper deep as in the ocean, and they are often filled with dust and *débris,* picked up by the hand of the whirlwind, and floated to distant shores. There is a theory that the air holds the history of the world by the changed position of its particles produced by sound or motion. Every voice and every act is chronicled in this invisible book. The same is true of this subtle power. There may come from a heart an influence like the breath of an iceberg or a sirocco of passion, or a holy peace fragrant of heaven, which will fall on men like the benediction of Jesus, never to die. An idea, a pulse, may go out from a single man and other hearts may set toward it until a current is formed; a gulf stream is created which may roll through the ages.

This power is in ratio to the talent God has given us: intellect, wealth, position, health, suffering. Many are sighing, "Oh, could I stand in some place of prominence; had I wealth and fame," but they should not forget all this means power, and power means effect, and both mean accountability. Many are repining at their humble estate, feeling "I have no talent, no genius; my life must be lowly, a life of toil and menial service; it is no matter to the world how I live or when I die;" when the fatal mistake and the secret of such discontent is the selfish ideal of life which shines in the soul. It is not the abundance, but the quality which is the criterion of success; not the amount, but the kind of power we possess. That little leaf which breaks off in the wind and falls faded and withered at your feet did not live in vain; it spread itself to the storm, sheltered the tree, sucked in the sunshine, sent a thrill of life to the great heart, laid itself out in solid wood, put its sweetness into fruit, cast its little shadow, was a thing of beauty, and at last laid down its life for the tree, and the world was richer for it. It may be but a little place at some lowly fireside or in society, but there are hearts nearer to yours than to any other in the world, and you must live for them. If the service be unto Him who died for us and rose again, its identity will not be lost, nor its glory pale amid the brightest stars of the firmament. There are some men without great talent, but they shine, they fill the home with light, they shine in business, and in the church; the light may be but a rush-light, but it is reflected from heart to heart like the rays of the morning; it will never go out; it will always be light, a widening sheet of light through the ages. And there are others we must measure as men do the mountains of the moon, by the length of the shadows they cast; it may be only a little shadow, but it is very long.

You call it a lowly place where you stand, and think you do but little good or ill. Remember it is among souls you live. You may be moulding some little heart which will rise to a place of power and sway the destinies of nations; you may be touching some hand which will turn the tide of history; you surely are touching some regal natures which will live on in thought and memory when the lamps of the sky are burned out. And this power we can never recall; it is gone forever. We make an image on that nature, but we may not wipe it out; not even the breath of prayer can bleach it; we might be glad to blot it out with our blood; we may send a spirit into the heart of our loved one which will resist the love of God; there may leap from our bosom in a moment of passion a fiery bolt which may shatter forever the hope and faith of our dearest friend; we cannot take back that word, that look, that sneer, it has gone into a nature which will never die; eternity will show the scars, if not the wrecks, of our power; in God's world there is no lowly place, no trifling act. David sang, "My heart shall live forever," and by his glorious minstrelsy it is throbbing on in many bosoms. Paul and Silas sang only in a dungeon, but their song is heard every night in some sad home, some lonely cell. Bunyan had a dream in Bedford jail and it has come to pass a thousand times.

There is sometimes a generous feeling in the nature of the most reckless, that if they do choose to go to ruin themselves, they do not want to drag others down.

If they are sceptics they do not want to blast the faith of their friends; they do not want loved ones to walk in their steps to the abyss; they do not want to rob them of their crown. It would take the heart of a devil to desire such results; even when you are in sin you do not want an evil influence, you would rather save men; but you cannot avoid consequences; say what you will, you are linked to your fellow-men, and by all the force of your life and character you drag them down; your very heart is beating against their purposes, against their faith; you can only repeat yourself; it is your image which is photographed upon them. It is a fact of science that every burning substance shining through a lens casts its own peculiar spectrum. If it is sin or vice in your heart it will cast upon their souls the black spectra of hell and you cannot help it. You do not wish to make your image as you are, but as you might be, and very few there are who do not intend some time to seek this higher life; but you cannot gather up the power for evil which every day is going out from you. Besides, this selfish life dies hard; it grows every day; pride cannot crush it, nor poverty starve it; death cannot kill it; it is the "ruling passion, strong in death."

We cannot begin too early, and even then we cannot conquer alone. The cross must lift you. Your eye will be filled with your own glory, your own star, and circle around and adjust the universe to it, unless this Star of Bethlehem arises upon your soul. Look upon that vicarious love which bows in Christ and bleeds upon Calvary. Can you not resolve to live unto Him whose love for you was unto death?

III

THE ENDLESS LIFE

"Or loweth the ox over his fodder?"

JOB vi. 5.

THE ox has all it wants. Why should he low? He has forgotten the yoke, the furrow, and the lash. He has no worry about the morrow. He does not fret about the future. He lies down at night content with his cud, and lets the world roll on until morning.

Job was another style of being. He could not be easy with his great troubles. He had too great a mind to rest, and his soul had too much in it to be content with the coarse fare of the ox.

Did anyone ever stand on the bank of a deep flowing river and look over to the other side without thinking of another river whose dark tide he soon must stem, but over which hangs a mist into which he peers, but cannot penetrate? The first time you stood by the sea and looked away over the waters and waters, and watched the ships go out of sight, and thought on until you almost doubted your geography, did you not think of another ocean, where, too, you had seen ships go out of sight, floating away until they drowned, and you were almost afraid there was no other shore, and no

35

THE GOSPEL MIRROR

"Green hills far away"? Haven't you, some summer night, watched the stars and seen them sinking, like bright ships, in the sea of space, and said, "Oh, is there any world among them where I shall go when I go from this? or will I never go from this? Will I go down in a few summers more, and they burn on forever?" The poet helps out the teaching of the star:

> "The star that sets
> Beyond the western wave is not extinct;
> It brightens in another hemisphere
> And gilds another evening with its rays."

Is there one who has not wrestled with the grim shadow from the grave as he has looked into its clay mouth, opening and shutting with awful silence and cruelty? Schiller's idea is a dubious gospel, but better than nothing. He says, "Death happens to all and cannot therefore be evil."

One thing seems certain, that if there is any existence at all after death, it must be more and greater than this. The word of science is progress, and so, if this life is not the end of being, it is the start of greater being. If there is anything, there is something vastly more than we have experienced. But shut up the Bible and say, is there anything? Men of all ages and races, the greatest that ever thought, as well as the most stupid, have thought there is.

THE ENDLESS LIFE

Look at this outside crystal palace of hope which shines on every shore, and say how assuring it is, and what its worth to virtue. It is not easy to estimate just how much certainty is necessary to a pure life and character. Only a "perhaps" has more power over some men than an absolute faith in a revealed future has over others. Rude and ignorant minds or souls sunken in vice and sensuality must have a future close by to affect them. Their day of judgment must be to-morrow to be of any use. The reward or penalty must be sure and swift. As people grow purer and more cultured they take in a longer range; they see and feel the distant coming joy or sorrow. There have been souls, like Socrates and Aurelius, who, out of only a cloudy "perhaps," could wring a hope strong enough to hold them, and bright enough to lead them like a star. Froude has a curious idea that the perfect belief in immortality is liable to abuse. Certain it is that men walk under a belief through which breaks an apocalypse which ought to shock them into holy pains. They would be indignant if you were to question their faith. "Do you think I am a pagan?"—and yet they are utterly without conscience in daily life; while there have been pagans who translated their own dim thoughts into visions and clean lives, and clung to a doubt until it turned, I believe, into the gate of heaven.

This is only a segment of the great suggestive argument for a future life. It is the argument which grows out of the nature of the soul's desires; its own instinctive prophecies of a future being; this is the ladder which we push out of us into the deep unseen, upon which our hopes may climb, and which we would shake and test to see if there is anything solid against which it can lean, so that, if possible, we may help the faith or open the eyes which have grown so dim they do not see the steps let down from heaven; while to awake a startling doubt in the mind of some who believe so much, and are moved so little, might prove a means of grace.

There is awakened in the mind an expectation of more life than this by the improvability of mind; it does something to-day, it can do more and better to-morrow. In its infancy the instinct of the insect or animal has the start, and yet how soon and how far behind it is left in the race. No eagle goes into competition with another to beat it in its evolutions. No boss-beaver is needed to oversee the job and show apprentices how to work up to the specifications. No beaver genius ever broke out with a new invention for a toboggan, or applied for a patent for a new style of dam. The bees have no schools for wax-work, or the birds for nest-building or music. They all do as their fathers did, and their old-fogy notions cannot be beaten out of them. There is no growth, no evolution toward anything higher. You may teach your dog or horse a few tricks, and the parrot another set of words, but, as you look them in the eye, you feel there is no growth of mind; or, if you claim there is, it is within an iron circle of instinct whose limits are soon reached. But look now into your own soul and tell me its limitations—how far it can go, and how high it can climb; look over all that man has done, in the mechanics, in art, in science; go over this world and look at the machinery, in the shops, on the seas, on the road—mind in wood and iron, mind on wheels, mind with wings; go through the art galleries and see the pictures—mind in paint; beauty, thought, passion, in marble; go through the universities and museums and see the trophies of mind, relics of its researches, jewels for its crown. Now all this from the rude things of the fathers is the picture of race growth, and that is only the image of one mind's growth, from the toys of the baby to the achievements of a man.

Yes, but what has this to do with immortality? Other things grow and die forever; but not before they reach maturity, and the evident end of their being. A summer here is long enough to make the most perfect rose, a head of wheat, or an apple; an orange and oleander must have a Florida. God gives a whale a thousand years to be a whale. Now put your boy in school and let his mind struggle up through the mysteries, and make its muscle by throes and victories; stimulate to effort by your love and smiles; hold up your prizes until he has passed through the primary, academy, and college, and has some knowledge and discipline, and what now? Have you not in all this awakened in your boy an expectation that he is to live on and do something in the world, enter some profession or business? What now, if you shall take him by the hand on the day of his graduation and say, "My son, this is all there is of life for you; to-morrow your reason will go out like a candle, your mind will be extinct. Good-by, my son, to-night, forever." What an absurdity your course if you know the end! What a mockery your prizes and tacit promises, what a cheat and sham, what an expensive piece of foolishness is it all, and what a father! And what, if he had ability to give him more life? Have you any idea that God can do that? Bring all other things to maturity, give all others time for development, and cut off a man in the pride of his being? The cheapest things, an insect, an ant, a bee, a bird, a flower, a tree, give all of them a chance to be what they were made for, and blot out the human mind after all this expense and pains and struggle, the costliest thing, the confessed masterpiece of His creation, in the earliest stages of its development?

You go to the great man who has had the best chance, the finest body and the brain as its instrument, and a long life for study and work, and ask him how it all seems to him. Have you done your best, written your best things in science, made your best steam-engine, your grandest organ, your finest painting, sung your sweetest song, your choicest poesy, your noblest thought, or done the most heroic deed of which you are capable? Hark: "I am only a boy picking up pebbles on the shore of the great ocean; coarse and rude are all these things to those I feel within me." They are toys compared with the things which throw their shadows on his thoughts and redden them with hope. "Just give me time," exclaims Newton, "and see what I can do."

How often, as the musician has sung the sweet melodies which gushed up from the soul, he has felt the distant tones of another strain which has so bewitched him that he floated through the noisy crowds unconscious as did old Mendelssohn. How many little ones in their lowly work have said, "Oh, I can do something different from this if I only had time. I feel it is in me; I feel powers just breaking loose like a bird's wing from the shell."

The poet-author of "Saul" was forty years old when the vision rose in him. General Banks said he graduated from a university which had a water-wheel at the bottom and a bell on top, and if, in a few years, against odds, a cobbler can be a senator like Wilson, a tanner a General Grant, a ploughman a Burns or a Cincinnatus, a clerk a Horace, a hostler a Defoe, a slave a Terence, a weaver a Columbus, what may not any man be if only he have time? How that human mind, in a poor weak body, or brain wrestling at its daily task in the study or studio, driven on by an indomitable will, and writhing under criticism, might turn and cry out, "Give me time and see what I will do, how I will grow." Won't God give us time when it is so cheap, and costs no more for millions to live than one? Will God not give us time?

Closely allied to this evidence is that of the soul's unmet wants. It not only knows that its fairest works are poor and imperfect, and but shadows of what they ought to be, but feels their incompleteness. A man frets at imperfection, struggles to finish something, and so is forever building on to his house, or building it over. The greater his mind the less likely to be suited with its own creations. He feels there is something better, he tears up his manuscript and writes it over, and is never done. So it is with everything we have to do; we are soon cloyed; we want a new diet every day. To many poor souls the great joy of spring lies in the changes of fashion, something new to wear. A change. Nothing changes often enough to suit us, but the weather, and that is mostly for the worse. Oh, the "restless wanderers after rest!" Nothing right, nothing perfect, no climate, no shore, no palace, no Alhambra!

It is not so with the birds, not so with the fishes. Nothing that creeps or swims or flies or walks, but finds in its conditions enough, and praises its Maker with some sign or song of content; but he who stands as lord of creation is as full of unrest as a caged tiger. He is ever abroad. He is forever homesick. His dreamy eyes are on the distance. "He never is but always to be blest." Now is not this a fair prophecy of his soul that there is another life where his great soul shall be full and settle in content?

Men may argue: "Do you not teach that all this unrest is the result of sin; that its perversions are full of unrest; its lusts as full of torment as the dregs of its cup of misery?" True, there is great peace and content in the salvation from sin when the soul is at home in its God; but, with all that, the deeper the restless cry after a perfect life, a perfect joy, perfect beauty, a perfect home, and a perfect vision of God!

Again, it is affirmed all along the ages that man naturally has a hope of immortality. Even when, because of sin, conscience turns on him and changes that hope into a cloud of wrath full of lightnings, it only strengthens the proof, hence remorse is only a grim hope.

Then too, the dread of death, the instinctive clinging

to life, intimates it. We naturally love to live. Until life is poisoned with a great sorrow, until all that is in it is bitter and terrible and its very light hateful, or until by vice men crush their sensibilities and are wallowing brutes, or come to think they are by a brutal belief; until then, life is very sweet, and death an unwelcome visitor in all homes. The soul looks up into the face of God and asks to live. He who made it put that prayer in it, and can He blow it out forever?

The dread of being forgotten when we are gone is another and a unique instinct of this strange being. The forget-me-not is in every human breast. The plaintive cry for remembrance comes from all lips. The earth is full of tombs, and every head-stone is this prayer. Men are ambitious to do heroic deeds, to write a great book, or to climb to a great place, not only to be seen and admired now, but to be immortal on earth, to haunt the world with their ghostly selves when they are dead; even this desire is a shadow of this longing to live after death. "Since I must die, then, as the next thing to it, let me live in the memory of men." This craving, too, is the shadow of another life, in that it intimates that we shall be living somewhere, and so have a vital and deathless interest still in the affairs and people of the earth. How can he otherwise wish to live in name if he, himself, shall have ceased to be?

Then, through all this there comes the yearning after

an endless life itself. Is it not so? Do not all men who have lifted their eyes to that horizon, and once entertained the thought, cling to it until it is a prayer? And why wonder, then, that such mighty instincts have crystallized into a universal belief, unless, indeed, that faith has floated down from the beginning? Dr. Dick says it was believed by the ancient Egyptians, the Persians, the Phœnicians, the Scythians, the Celts, the Druids, the Assyrians.

"The ancient Scythian believed that death was only a change of habitation, and the magicians of Babylon, Media, Assyria, and Persia admitted the doctrine of eternal rewards and punishments." All know that Plato and Socrates held the doctrine of the soul's immortality. So their poets have written of the Hesperian Gardens, and the Elysian Fields, and Pindar, the great lyric poet, sang, four hundred years before Christ came, of this strange hope:

> "The islands of the blest, they say,
>   The islands of the blest,
> Are peaceful and happy by night and day,
>   Far away in the glorious west.
>
> They need not the moon in that land of delight,
>   They need not the pale, pale star,
> The sun he is bright by day and by night,
>   Where the souls of the blessed are.

THE GOSPEL MIRROR

"They till not the ground, they plough not the wave,
  They labor not, never, oh never!
Not a tear do they shed, not a sigh do they heave,
  They are happy forever and ever.

"Soft is the breeze, like the evening one,
  When the sun hath gone to his rest,
And the sky is pure and clouds there are none
  In the islands of the blest.

"The deep, clear sea, in its mazy bed,
  Doth garlands of gems unfold;
Not a tree but it blazes with crowns for the dead,
  Even flowers of living gold."

What a song for a heathen!

We find this hope on every shore; among the old Moors and Mexicans, as also among our Indians who looked for a paradise in the west where nature glowed with an eternal sunset, their Happy Hunting Ground. All this, too, independent of any revealed hope or faith.

Then, akin to all this, is our love for the dead. It is not so with the animal. The bird may flutter a little about its dead mate; the bereaved cow may low her grief for a few hours, but all soon forget and evidently cease to love.

One has said: "Why was it that the Aborigines of our own country were wont to send messages of love by the wild forest birds to their kindred in the spirit land? Why do some of the heathen kneel annually at the graves of their dead and whisper, 'I love you still'? But with what unearthly tenderness do we still cling to those we knew and loved, but who have passed from our society to return no more."

All these voices in me blend into one mighty cry, one great hope, and is there no reality?

God puts out the eye of the fish in Mammoth Cave where there is no light. There is no other destiny for the ox; no other heaven but the green meadow. He has no organ in him for any higher life. He never lifts his head with longing toward the skies. Would God not be as kind to us? Would He plant this longing for my dead, and for life forever, this longing for beauty and perfection, if there be no such blessed reality? Would He not be as kind to me as He is to a fish and put out this hope in me if there is no life, if my loved ones are gone out forever? Surely, if He were good! Surely, if He is God!

We are often saved by hope. Why, then, would this hope of immortality not be a benevolent illusion which we may follow with bright eyes until the last, even if there be no answering life to come? Besides, we never would know the difference. We go to sleep with the smile on our face and never wake up; that is all; we never would know the cheat, for, of course, no one can come back with an *exposé* of the sweet dream. Ah, no! we shudder at the statement of this indictment against the Creator; that He could organize a lie in this wondrous structure of the soul, and then amuse and stimulate us with an everlasting fraud. And how, if He were such a Being would He desire our happiness in the creation of a false hope, or expect to culture us with a delusion? No, God cannot mock us; there must be another shore.

But one may say, "There are illusions in this life; the world is full of illusions. Even as the boy chases the rainbow to find its gold and crimson over in the orchard; as poor wanderers on the desert have hunted a mirage until their tongues cracked with thirst and the waving palm-trees mocked their dying eyes; so we chase appearances and get bubbles. People laugh at us, and we laugh, if we can, to hide our disappointment. We say the cheat sharpened our wits, and the running did us good. We say, 'Better to have loved and lost, than never to have loved at all.' We take it kindly when we are young, but the joke is serious when we are old and our feet tired." Yes, there are illusions here. A poet has said,

"This world is all a fleeting show
For man's illusion given,"

and that statement is false, even if he rhymes the last word with heaven; they are not "given." God did

48

not make our eyes to see illusions, but to see things as they are. It is not God's fault if we mistake morphine for quinine, even if we sleep in death for the illusion; nor is it His fault if we believe the world is flat, the centre of all things, around which the sun revolves; or that a man comes to think he is the centre, and all things are for him—perhaps the most common of all illusions, and the hardest to cure. No, it is not God's fault; it is the result of our ignorance, or our sin, or that of another; and when both maladies are cured the illusions are dissolved, the clear brain and the pure heart rise above the mocking mists, discerning spirits and breaking the spell of the magician.

But when all these illusions are dispelled, when men have wrestled with these mysteries, and come the nearest to mastering them, this other "illusion," if so you call it, or "hope," has stood out the strongest and the grandest. Often when the greatest minds have wrestled with that and tried to prove it also an illusion; tried to master this hope as a superstition, whether in the alembic of the mind, or in the retort of science, it has risen in their souls like the fabled bird from the ruin and ashes to soar in light. The more they have sought to analyze and test it; the more they have struggled with it, to crush it from the soul, or to prove it divine, the more vivid and blessed has it become, until, like Jacob's angel, its face has come out in the morning, and the hills are gay with breaking light.

So this illusion, if such it is, remains after the clearest research and the utmost pains; and if it prove true, and our hope be real, it accounts for, and compensates, and swallows up all other illusions; they all come to pass in the effulgence of that life. Otherwise, all life on earth is an illusion, which, with its mysteries, culminates in a stupendous fraud.

True, men cherish false hopes and notions of the world to come, absurd, maybe, as those of the Indian's hunting ground, but the illusions are the necessary results of our finite minds, and, however wild or crude or earthlike, they will be more than met in the mighty realities of that immortal life which God cannot crowd into our baby brains. As we come up into that life it may be like a young eagle broken out of its shell to find its dark egg-dreams lost in its sweep of wing out in the deep air, and its clear eye full of the gleams of the sun. Life yonder will drown in its blessedness all our hopes!

I want to point you to a scene yonder over the hills of Gilead. You see the rugged form of the old prophet of the desert, and by his side the ploughman; they pass down the slopes of Jericho to the river. The smitten waters wait for them to cross, and, yonder on the other shore, they walk on toward the mountains conversing together, one of them on the brink of heaven, when

suddenly, says the record, "Behold there appeared a chariot of fire, and horses of fire, and parted them both asunder; and Elijah went up by a whirlwind into heaven."
We may not try to paint that glorious going. With the
fifty staring prophets who stood on the other side of the
Jordan, we may strain our eyes after the ascending prophet, or cry, with the bereft Elisha, "My father, my father!
The chariot of Israel and the horsemen thereof!" We
know not to what bright shore the fiery horses drew him,
but he survived the journey. Peter, James, and John
saw him alive nine hundred years after in the clear light
of the Transfiguration. That gorgeous ascension stands
out against the sky of holy history; what did it mean
but immortality?

Oh, may you take that mighty faith which comes floating down from the chariot with the mantle of Elijah,
wear it next your soul through the storms of doubt and
trouble,—and, with it, like Elisha, smite the cold waves
of your Jordan and make that other shore, even if no
fiery horses are in sight.

However bright or certain, these rays converge and
are lost in the effulgence of glory breaking above the
cross of Jesus, and, as we gaze, a voice comes down
from its depths of light: "Let not your heart be
troubled: ye believe in God, believe also in me. In my
Father's house are many mansions: if it were not so, I
would have told you."

51

IV

THE SPIRIT OF THANKSGIVING

"And on the fourth day they assembled themselves in the valley of Berachah; for there they blessed the Lord: therefore the name of the same place was called, The valley of Berachah, unto this day."

II. CHRONICLES, xx. 26.

THERE had been a fast-day in Israel. The wild hordes of Mount Seir had made a league with Ammon and Moab against Judah. Vivid accounts of the advancing host had come to King Jehoshaphat. He had no armies or allies to match that, so, in his fear and feebleness, he sought an alliance with heaven; he proclaimed a fast. "Even out of all the cities of Judah they came to seek the Lord." In tears and trembling they came. "And all Judah stood before the Lord, with their little ones, their wives, and their children." A great, pitiful prayer pleading in the voice of their king: "We have no might against this great company . . . neither know we what to do; but our eyes are upon Thee." Then the Spirit came upon Jahaziel, and he cried, "Be not afraid . . . for the battle is not yours, but God's. To-morrow go . . . stand ye still, and see the salvation of the Lord." So they went singing to meet

53

that barbarian host; the praises of God their battle-song. But the battle was over ere they came upon the scene. In an awful mutiny the foe had fallen,—the field was ghastly—the brook Jeruel ran with the blood of Seir, and the wild hills of Ziz were strewn with the dead. Now, laden with the spoils of the foe, they gathered in this valley of Berachah to celebrate their victory and glorify God. Hearty and unanimous must have been that grand thanksgiving! The songs of that jubilant host never died out of those listening rocks. The Te Deums of those glad hearts were made perpetual, for they christened the holy ground "The Valley of Blessing."

If during the year our own land had been shaken with the armies of Europe, if our lives and liberties had been in jeopardy, and, in an unequal contest, we had been victorious, driven the invader from our hearth-stones, and grown rich in his gold and armaments, then in the flush of such a victory, in the joy of rest from the horrors of war, would we pour out before heaven our gladdest songs upon this national thanksgiving. But we have said no adieus to loved ones going into the shock of battle. We celebrate no martial conquests. As we gather in our national Berachah there are about us no garments rolled in blood, no spoils of war, only the fruits of industry, only the spoils of the reaper, only the trophies of the Cross. But is not the harvest field as prolific

54

of praises as the field of blood? Are not the mild mercies of peace as sweet with heaven's favor as the red relics of war? Must our feet be fresh from some Red Sea to feel the rhythm of praise? Must our cymbals be silent until wakened by the wails of the drowning foe? Must the savage in our veins see scalps to start our songs? Shall not our valley be as grateful as Judah's Berachah? Or shall God be grieved to-day by only the cold fashion of a religious festival?

That was a true type of thanksgiving. It had its origin in a fast. If Judah, in her crisis, had not come mourning before God, that jubilee would not have been written in her history. Judah came through the valley of humiliation into the valley of blessing. So penitence is the prelude of praise. It has in it the spirit of divine reliance and alliance, the courage of faith, all the conditions of victory. There were times in the memories of some of us when our hearts were sick by hope deferred. At the call of our martyr President, the nation bowed in these places of prayer, wept over its sins, and threw itself on God; even before another battle there was light in the clouds of war; our soldiers felt it at the front, and gold went down in Wall Street. When a man or a nation puts away sin in honest tears there is put away the ground of distrust in God, so that even before the witness of pardon reaches the conscience, there springs up in the sorrow a faith which exults in

55

coming mercy, even as if its sign were radiant in the breast. Thus the fast begot faith, and to weary watchers in that awful night the stars came out, even before Grant went to Vicksburg, or Sherman rode to the sea. So the disaster which stuns a proud people to its knees oftener emits a brighter prophecy on its sky than what is called prosperity. From the "dust and ashes" springs a sturdy trust which lays hold of God for success. Who doubts that prophecy doubts the human heart, and all history human and divine.

Judah went from her knees, singing, to meet the foe. Her faith reversed the order of victory. England yet believes it was the breath of prayer which flung back from her shores the Spanish Armada; even as we, that the prayers of Delfthaven were the pilots of the Mayflower. Perhaps that little divine idea, clad in iron, the Monitor, floated through the nation's tears into Hampton Roads to meet the Merrimac, even as emancipation and victory were born in throes of contrition. Thus in all life, in the calamity which smites us low, in the bitterness of grief for sin, is begotten the truest trust, and the sweetest triumph. So often our direst extremity is God's best opportunity, and the Miserere ends in a Te Deum.

The spirit of penitence is the spirit of praise because of its humility. It is a feeling of unworthiness. The man to-day who looks back through the years of his

THE SPIRIT OF THANKSGIVING

life for causes of thanksgiving, if it is with a vivid sense of his personal sins before God, has such a humiliating estimate of his deserts that he reckons every benefit a gratuity, and a claim upon his gratitude. His tears magnify God's gifts. His vision is thus clarified as it sweeps the landscape across which he has come, until hill and dale, rocks and trees, yes, even the wild gorge where his feet bled, and the very storms which swept over him, all are retouched and bathed in this mellow light of penitence, and it seems a masterpiece of mercy. Have you not felt this lowly spirit transfigure your past, gleaning out of a varied experience unrecorded benefits, lighting up forgotten joys until every holy spot was streaming to the skies in fiery incense; gathering around you like a magician the haunting faces of even spiritual gifts, which came smiling, but went grieving from an ungrateful heart; bringing back from the dead blessings buried and unsung, until it seemed as if all the loving-kindness of life had come in for a thanksgiving, and the humble soul beneath its weight of memories was dumb with praise? To such a spirit the common mercies of life are fragrant of heaven. Daily bread has something of the sanctity of manna. The very raiment is interwoven with golden threads of Providence. Little things along the pathway are thoughts of God and full of tongues.

But some there are who take blessings of every sort

as a matter of course; take all, take everything they can get as if it were their right and the Almighty were largely in their debt for having brought them into being. They take the rich gifts of life without common civility, and as if nothing were good enough for their dainty dignities, and they were conferring an amazing favor on their Maker and the universe for consenting to live. Rich or poor, they are too great for gratitude. No surprises of Providence can equal their expectations. Selfish and self-righteous, they scarcely need pray as it is said a devout Scotchman was wont to, daily, for "a better opinion of himself." They have not seen God's face through their sins, and so learned to grieve for them. Hence this lofty spirit which only pities itself for its misfortunes, and has no tears left for its guilt, minifies its mercies and magnifies its miseries, "Writes," it has been said, "its injuries in marble, and its benefits in dust." In its ingratitude it gathers up all the garbage of its past, the fag ends of every disaster, drags its muck-rake up and down the bright streams of life, and from the heaped-up rubbish of trouble, sends the vile effluvia to heaven! It is the morning and evening sacrifice. Its vulture throat croaks requiems. The bells which call to its service are tolling; they never ring out a thanks-giving. A penitent spirit exults in the discovery of its fault, and in hope of remedy. The other is ungrateful, and in all its repining, ignores sin as the only real evil and root of bitterness. Thus, in the retrospection of this hour, if a true soul cannot be thankful in view of its own responsible past and present, it can at least exult if it has branded the destroyer of its peace.

If we cannot be thankful for what is so bad—we call it corruption—at the caucus, at the ballot-box, in social life, and in politics, in all trades and professions—but ours—thankful for bribery, stealing, perjury, incest, and murder, we can be grateful that there seems to be moral sense enough to feel the cancerous nature of such vices in the vitals of the nation. True, we cannot do penance for millions; our vicarious sufferings may count little for a great country, even if pure as those whose shadow fell upon the Holy City, but there is hope in that so many hearts ache to-day as if they were to blame: ache over the spirit of lawlessness which reigns in our homes, our public schools, on our streets, from villages to the great cities; law, which is the hedge about our holiest things and the guardian angel of our liberties, whose jewelled hand holds the flag over all our country; ache at the lust of money, which rides rough-shod over the rights of the poor, thunders its vandal trains through the heart of our Sabbath, and tariff or no tariff, seems bound to own the earth; ache at this other lust, which, with leprous feet, tracks its mire into the home and halls of legislation and strangles all love, hissing at the name of virtue and marriage; ache over the awful gulf of intemperance,

59

at which all good men grow pale and turn away with their ears too full of its wails to think of a song.

Yet more, your very souls have burned at a rumor that a citizen sold, yes sold, his vote; sold what is the sign of manhood and liberty; sold what was worth more than all that such a man had left, all of him which would bring a price in any market; sold, like Esau, his birthright for a mess of pottage; and that there were men bold and bad enough to buy. To sell a ballot, the voice, the hand, the will, the right of a freeman, is a crime next to treason. That ballot was born at Lexington, and christened out of the heart of half a million of our bravest. It was steeped in their agonies. It has the smell of fire and the sound of cannon in it. The ballot means as much as the flag; nay, the flag is in it, and he who drags the one into the mire is as much a traitor as he who hauls down the other. I wish a little section of Shiloh were in every ballot so that men would handle it with care, otherwise that it would shatter as a shell the profane hand which bought or sold it. That righteous anger which you felt proves that you know where lie the foundations of this Republic; that you are sensitive to this vice which uncrowns the only king of this monarchy, the white or black man; that you feel that iniquity may prove our ruin. This is written on the tombs of all the old nations, for they are buried. One has said, "However it is with individual, national souls have been uniformly damned, and the earth is one vast gehenna of nations." More are evidently on their way to judgment. Never did a nation fall, but by iniquity. Private vice is soon public corruption, and then it goes fast, by anarchy or conquest. In an old classic republic, so often quoted, for one hundred and seventy years there was no divorce. Woman was the type of purity, and the family the home of virtue. As long as the hearth-stone, which was the basis of the whole fabric, was sacred, Rome was solid as her seven hills. But Grecian literature and manners, and Asiatic vices were the insidious scouts of the Gothic host. Intellect was cultured. Statesmen were there, historians and poets, but not the sturdy virtues of the days when Cincinnatus left the plough for the helm of state. So Greece was in chains when Demosthenes was the orator of Athens. So sin told the story of old Assyria. It crept beneath the gates of Babylon before Cyrus. Its wails are in Judah's harp on the willows of the Euphrates.

Can we not hear among other nations a rustling as of autumn leaves, and almost feel the fierce winds of iniquity which must take them away? I would not seem to strike a dirge to-day, but will not our Gloria fit more hearts if in this minor mode? For he who can get solid comfort out of this world's affairs, and they are our affairs, is a bee which can suck honey out of some ugly flowers. But we have had loud teaching in the crimson story of old Spain; and if it be dinned into our dull ears by the voice of our victorious cannon, all the cost of the war and the twenty millions for the Philippines will be cheap tuition. Chains of ignorance and standing armies will not hold slaves forever. Bull-fights and bigotry will not always divert immortal men. Superstition and lust and gold will not do on earth for the religion and civilization of the Cross. And we, no more than old Spain, or Italy, or Austria, or Russia, or the bloody empire of the crescent, can long thrive on any other diet than righteousness.

So if we have seen enough of the grim things of the year to repent, it is good reason for thanksgiving.

This penitent spirit gives thanks most for God's favor. In the luxuries of nature and life it will rise above all gifts in the joy of its own life in Him; even in loss and sorrow will soar above a desert and exult in the possession of the great Giver Himself. Said a Christian man who had lost his property, "When I was rich I had God in all things, now I have all things in God." It is a spirit which is grateful, not so much for what it has, but for what it is in Him; so its springs break out within and are fed from the Infinite. The other spirit is self-sufficient and looks without, ignoring the "Father of Lights." Such a man is saying, in feeling if not in words, "True, I have a home, food, raiment, but it is by my own hard hands, my own skill and foresight, no one ever helped me to a dollar," and "All this is mine and thanks to nobody. I haven't seen any manna about my doors. I haven't picked up any gold which shows the mint of heaven. I haven't fished any silver out of the sea, like Peter;" forgetting that power to work, the mind and life, were greater benefactions than the gold. Such a man ought at least to be thankful that he was not born an oyster instead of a man—in some respects the change would have been slight.

How many of our great men, who may recognize God in the etiquette of a yearly thanksgiving, are like the boaster of Babylon, "My own arm hath gotten all this; my genius, my statesmanship has piloted the ship of state," when, perhaps it was in spite of all God kept her in the billows. Often the pride is harder than the wrath of man to turn into praise. Pope Hadrian wrote an inscription on a college he had built: "Utrecht planted me, Lorraine watered me, but Cæsar gave the increase." Some pious wit wrote beneath this blasphemy, "It seems that God did nothing for this man." But let the light go out of the home; let the fruit be blasted, and the harvest fail, and all are charged back on a mysterious Providence. How prone the heart of him who appropriates all the good, and only remembers God for convenience or blame in the day of trial, who credits all the gains to his own genius and charges up his common woes and his own faults to the Almighty!

THE GOSPEL MIRROR

Really, there is something for gratitude in every life, and no lot is without its compensations. "The ugliest trades," declares Douglas Jerrold, "have their moments of pleasure; now if I were a grave-digger or a hangman, there are some people I could work for with a great deal of enjoyment." Surely there is good in reach of all; only the mischief is, the crumbs of comfort are not picked up by those in whose lot they fall. It is always in some other calling or estate they look like grains of gold. "Oh," says Emerson, "if the rich were only as rich as the poor think they are." So this spirit not only forgets God, but blindly stumbles over its own joys, gloating with green eyes on other's good, and covetous of all. It is hard and barren as a rock of praises. It must be divinely smitten to be a Horeb breaking forth in crystal streams which ripple their own thanks. Tell such a discontented one of any favor and he finds a fault. Every mercy he matches with a wrong, and evens up all life with his own gall. If the weather is fair, the roads are rough; if the harvest was great, the market is dull; if the sun is bright, there are spots upon it, and this morbid spirit magnifies those spots with its evil eye until it shivers through the world under their shadow. Reckon up for such a man all his mercies; read off the mighty aggregate; glean all life, and roll the figures in upon his selfish soul; but you cannot make him grateful by arithmetic any more than you can make a tramp a patriot by travel. He might, perhaps, stop on such a day as this, for thanksgiving, if he thought the President had a right to appoint it, but at best his memorial for a year's loving-kindness would be a few frigid thoughts, a heap of stones for his Ebenezer, or a fat turkey for his own dinner.

I might to-day build a monument before his eyes, its foundations laid in the deep ages of geology; fountains of oil, mountains of coal, the iron and the gold which God treasured up for him in the beginning; upon that put his own life with all its wealth of love and hope; this great bright home, free government, free conscience, his marvellous body and soul, and I might crown the shining obelisk with God's unspeakable gift; around all breaking the joys of time and the great immortality, and write in jewels on every side of the Colossus, "God is love"; but as well make a picture of an old pyramid of Egypt unless his stony heart has melted in repentance for sin. Anthracite coal cannot warm an ungrateful heart, nor rivers of oil lubricate the tongue of a mummy. The spirit of praise must be born in throes of penitence.

A true spirit of praise in a nation will rejoice in what it is at heart, in faith in God and in righteousness more than in what it has of material splendor. These outward things in which we glory, our industries, our great cities, may be sources of evil. This tendency to great centres

65

tends to corruption, masses of men and fierce competition; makes vast corporations which infringe on the individual, and control legislation, politics, and the trade of the country. Here, too, generate the social evils and breed all vices. The literature, fashions, life of the great city throb out through the railroad and telegraph, and saturate and control the country. So it is that "Paris is France," and life throughout the nation hollow as the earth beneath that wicked city. So London is England; Berlin, Germany; so Boston, New York, Philadelphia, Chicago, New Orleans, and San Francisco are America. The nation is full of the life of these great cities. So our ground of boasting is not so much what we possess in material or mental wealth, as what we are in spiritual life in these great hearts of the commonwealth, for that is the secret and gauge of our popular government.

Separated Church and State we have, at least in theory, but we cannot divorce religion and politics in a republic any more than in a theocracy. We know that talent and physical science are no guarantees of peace or liberty. You cannot dam up the Niagara of intemperance with college diplomas. You cannot soothe the riots of discontent with lotions of literature. You cannot ride down Anarchy and Atheism with your iron horses. Our danger is not "Imperialism." Our foes do not wear crowns. They are too low browed. They are the things which breed and fester and crawl and hiss; corruption cannot be killed by cannon. We may go faster than the fathers, but what is the use if we go nowhere? We have left the homespun and the stage-coach; we ride in palace cars, go by steam and electricity, and think in the same swift fashions, but how much have we advanced beyond the old Puritan conscience? We cannot outwit sin by logic nor outflank lust by standing armies; we cannot pump iniquity out of politics by Corliss engines, nor show the devil out of the world with our electric stars. Our very prosperity has often turned us away from the Giver, and we have served the creature more than the Creator. And shall it come to pass with us as a people that it will be written on our tomb, "Gone with the nations which forget God?" We enthrone the empty agencies so much and cry, "These be thy gods." Our guns, our battle-ships, our Navy, our Army, our Sampsons, our Deweys, and our Manillas, our victories! But, yet, above our hands and genius, beyond nation and nature, this real spirit of praise mounts up in her own chariot and will not stop this side the throne. Past all agencies and angels, by thrones and powers, until the last creature is far below, in the "excellent glory," alone she bows before the "Father of Lights" and sobs out her thanksgiving, a doxology to the great Giver of all.

This spirit, too, is full of hope. "Long as I live," said David, "will I praise thee." He knew not what was in reserve, what disaster might uncrown him and send him out of his palace, but he turned his face toward the skies and shouted through the ages, "Long as I live will I praise Thee." So if, to-day, you and I, while remembering the tender mercies of the patient God, do mourn most for the sins which have grieved Him, our hearts are surely growing warm with a hope born of faith which looks through all clouds singing, "Long as I live will I praise Thee." As our fathers in darker days bent in tears and saw light through them, so in this spirit, in spite of all untoward things, we will hope for our country.

One man may wring a drop from strata below the desert, and tower like the palm-tree. Some see light in the mysteries of business, and tariffs, and trusts. Some see signs of speedy victory and peace, and find music in the roar of the cannon. Some of us exult in the fruits of "Cuba libre!" Some of us find causes of song in the closer bonds with the mother country, in spite of poor surveys and Alaska gold; and some in arbitration, if not in the Peace Congress; some of us in the brave, steady hand at the helm of state, and in the sighing for a purer national life. We have felt error desperate, as in the throes of some new agonies, even amid some defections of an old faith, out of which we know the truth will yet ride forth in the fair image of its king.

THE SPIRIT OF THANKSGIVING

New champions are rising up, correcting the hasty teachings of biased critics, digging from the tombs of old critics living vouchers, and raising the dead as witnesses. Differences in the Christian church are melting away, and the real white dove is hovering above her altars. Some dark spirits are on the wing, signs of our King's chariot seem coming up the sky. The East must be full of day. True, there are bad things which ought to be dead, and our dailies are staggering with the weight of crime and woe. But the good is too much to be told, and too common to be appreciated. Anyway, in this spirit we sing "We shall live to praise Him." And so is it fatalistic to feel that we must outlive our foes? that there is too much historic history for this republic to go down? too many graves in this soil?—that God did not guide across the ocean those praying Pilgrims to bury them in freedom's grave? They were the pioneers of His purpose. Plymouth Rock is a promise. The crimson tracks of Valley Forge are promises. The graves of Gettysburg are promises. The mantles of the great prophets of liberty are in the air. Will not God find men to wear them?

We feel that He has not sent us into a valley of death like that of Balaklava, but into a "Valley of Blessing"— green blossoming trees of righteousness—homes of plenty and joy—sentineled as the garden of God, and watered as heaven is. So we but touch the trophies

69

of the year, the heaped-up spoils of earth, the fabrics of our hands, and the fallen mercies of heaven, in this, our national Berachah. We are glad that we exist and hope; but while we smile through our tears, faith sings amid the clouds, "Long as I live will I praise Thee."

V

EDUCATION AND CHARACTER

GOD'S method of all life and help shows that He has progress in mind. With all His generosity there is this strict economy: divine strength is never given to any man until he needs it. God encourages bigger cups by filling to the brim those we empty. He does not give a baby a man's muscle; an infant Hercules is a monster. God, like a wise Father, gives us strength, not on the endowment plan, or we would squander it, but in installments as we need and appreciate it. He does not carry spendthrifts; He won't waste his patrimony on tramps; He does not endow laziness. The man who undertakes to sponge his living out of God will soon have to shift for himself and get his meals elsewhere. "He that reapeth receiveth wages."

The very structure of mind shows that man is made for advancement. His curiosity, his growing ability and intimations of hope! Just as the birds are made not only for their element, but are given wing-feathers and pinions—set for forward motion—God never made a bird to fly backward! So, remember you are organized

71

for advancement; every bone and bulging muscle and fledgling thought and drop of blood is preaching progress; that is the way your wing-feathers are placed— every function and organ set for going.

And, too, God encourages man by hiding the future, so that only one duty, one obstacle, comes out at a time. What if all were opened now by the parting of the mystic veil? Would you thank an angel to show you to-night all the discouragements? No, nor would I want him to disclose all the visions of victory, even by an apocalypse. It would rob one of the very qualities needed to win, and make one an imbecile. What if there were no slack chains between the loaded cars of a freight-train? No engine on the road could budge them. But it has only to start one and then another, until it is pulling thirty or forty cars up the grade. So, if there are duties and up-grades ahead, do not forget that they are all to be met, one by one. And if there are surprises of trial, there will be in such a prepared mind surprises of strength, even reserves of which you were unconscious. If there is an order to go against the Midianites, even if there is no visible angel, there will be dew on the fleece.

I know that men deify intellect. They canonize thinkers. Smartness has a thicker mantle than charity. Minerva beats the Pope. All sorts of vices are condoned in all men, but ministers, on account of mental greatness. A talented rascal wins laurels and suffrages, and goes to

EDUCATION AND CHARACTER

Congress; otherwise he gets into jail. Men will forgive anything but stupidity. Not that they glorify vice. Vice, stark naked, like a snake, has few friends and no admirers; but give it the serpent's wisdom and an angel's face and it is so charming. So the Devil and his novelists, whatever else they do with their hero, crown him with brains, and the book sells. So, idolizing intellectual greatness, we culture our child's head and let his heart get on, like his stomach, as best it can. And yet the world worships brains for what they are worth. It has no laurels for deadheads. It glorifies artists, inventors, scientists, discoverers. It weighs men by the amount they lift. It calculates the loftiness of a man's genius by the height of the position to which that genius has raised him. It measures the convolutions of his brain by his bank account. Success is the universal criterion of calibre. Hence we are often likely to substitute success for excellence; to aim at success, to put the accidental for the intrinsic, and the result is an accelerating degradation.

There are people who educate their children because it is the fashion. It is a shame to be ignorant. They want them to shine, so they mould them in the fashionable mode and choose those branches and schools which promise this end. The children are apt pupils and graduate at last in just those accomplishments. Shining is success. A bit of phosphorus blazes more than a diamond and is so much cheaper. Hence when the goal is success instead of merit, the inevitable tendency is to the superficial in mental culture and to the false in character.

We get the same conclusion with any other object as the ideal. Let one train himself for any profession with the mere idea of rising in it, winning fame or money, and he will lower the quality of the standard, and study methods of success instead of its principles. He will become the dodging servant of a shifting goal. Thus we get politicians for statesmen, and shams and quacks in all professions. Hence the great idea of education is simply to seem the most rather than to be the most possible, and let success follow, or failure.

In these days, if a man wants an education he will get it. His heart on fire is genius which will forge expedients and outwit hardship and any toil. But you may do everything and his friends do everything and the State do everything; put up buildings, open libraries, and if he has no desire, there is no use. You must by some wizard art evoke his slumbering fancy, wake up his mind, get his eye on the goal, like the youth of the old Excelsior, and break the magnetism of every other charm. He must want it as Jacob wanted Rachel, as Caleb wanted Hebron, as men want high office. Otherwise you cannot by any degrees or millinery keep up any permanent interest in it. You might as well try by a galvanic battery to make an athlete out of a corpse. So many want easy things. They are tired. They have

74

no gimp in them. They didn't cry when they were babies and never got into mischief; they were good because they were tired. They never hurry, never run after a train, they seem to be ever looking for a good place to sit down. Young men, too; they act as if they thought the world a great machine and God the motive power, and that all they have to do is to sit on and ride.

Well, it is not easy to get an education; it never was easy; it was not meant to be. It is exhaustive, hard work to think, to commit to memory, to gain knowledge, to ferret out the secrets of nature, to dig among the roots of dead languages and wrestle with the posers of mathematics. It is easier to exercise the muscles at foot-ball or in a boat-race. I do not envy athletes, but if only the physical training and vim could, by some transfusion, even by throes of torment, pass into brain power and agility, what scholars, what prodigies, our athletes would become. Our colleges would break down by the over-production of eminent scholarship. But it is not easy. The unfolding of the mind is often at the start in pain; its forces are led out in tribulation; its blossoms are in crimson. The very word is suggestive, "discipline." No kindergarten object-lessons or Loisette patents can make it easy. The moment it is easy, it fails and is not education. An unknown ocean was forbidding when Columbus made his desperate venture. Astronomy was not easy when Gal-

ileo and Newton wrestled with the stars, nor chemistry
easy when Becher and Stahl sowed the old alchemy with
the germs of the great science and Galvani and Faraday
ploughed up its mysteries by the electric current. What
science is yet easy? What art? Is it music? Is it painting? Is it sculpture? Is literature? Is philosophy? Is
anything easy? Then don't do it. It is not worth your
while.

There is no place worth going to in this world or the
next, but has written over its narrow gate in crimson,
"Strive to enter in."

And yet the hard things had rich sequences and sweet
memories. Just think, when a boy you ploughed among
the stumps and were pounded and flung until sore and
lame at night; you raked after and bound the wheat
and picked the thistles out of your arms afterward;
there were bee-stings and stone-bruises, and you had cold
fingers when you picked the apples and husked the corn;
your heart ached over the puzzles in the old arithmetic,
and you often thought you saw some hard times; but
those things are rubies in your blood now, and you smile
as you look through the haze of years. The stumps are
gone; there are no thistles in the wheat, no frost on the
apples in the old orchard, and you sigh at the rosy picture
back there in the old home.

So the story of education is often the story of want,
and the hard mother of most of our inventions, necessity,

is its genius. True, there is now and then a mind which takes to it like a hound to the chase, keen and happy in its toil; works at it, as Bunyan wrote, for that "joy did bid him write," and which will catch fire at its chosen task and go aloft in its own chariots. And when this spirit is once awake it goes about the world with a question in its mouth. It cannot rest in the paradise of ease. You might as well entertain a Bengal tiger in a drawing-room or amuse an eagle with a swing perch in a cage. But most minds, at the start, must not only feel some coaxing angel of hope, but be chased by the pang of hunger and cold and nakedness, or feel the flaming sword of duty behind thrusting them out of some Eden into discipline for the work of life; but it is oftener yet men who have no Eden over which to sigh and no angel but that with which they wrestle for success who are the fittest candidates for intellectual labor and the most stalwart toilers of this world.

There is not a calling on earth so lowly but is glorified by a list of illustrious men; not a shop but bears on its walls their mighty heraldry. Eliot was a mechanic, Hood an engraver, Ben Jonson a bricklayer, Turner a barber, Hugh Wilber a stone mason; Herschel changed his violin for the telescope, Claude Lorrain his pastry oven for an artist's easel. Beethoven said Rossini had the stuff in him to make a good musician if he had only been well flogged when a boy. "Bruise them in." Thus men have made beauty for bread, and have turned even cries of hunger into ravishing music, and their rags into garments of praise.

So, too, the lowest places may become thrones of power. Indeed, humility is the condition of discovery. Pride is not only the badge but the imperative condition of ignorance. It is called "That never failing vice of fools." She struts her little round, her feet tangled in the meshes of error. Her lofty head cannot bow under the low gate to all God's realms of truth and beauty. In this world every insect and atom is an oracle, but we must stoop for its response; every rock is a Horeb, but cannot be smitten by an arrogant hand. Darwin confessed that he failed to understand an orchid, because in his pride he scorned the teaching of the labellum at the top; he had to get down on his knees to the flower. And so God often breaks his secrets to these lowly, but He never diadems the swollen head of pride. So Jeremy Taylor was at his shears, Elihu Burrett at his forge, and Carey on his shoe-bench when there fell on them the gift of tongues whose glorious babble has thrilled the world. Peter was fishing that morning when Christ called him. Elisha was ploughing when the old prophet called him to witness his glorious taking off, and the taint of the plough did not soil the mantle of Elijah. It is not the dirt on the clothes, but the thick clay on the conscience which hurts our respectability up yonder. In this high structure of education he climbs the highest who digs the lowest beneath its foundations.

But mere intellectual culture is not enough—the whole nature of man must be developed. One may fill a drunkard's grave in spite of his arithmetic or chemistry; he may dangle from the gallows like Ruloff, in spite of his philology. You can't cure lust by botany or hedge up the way to the pit by a college diploma. Fools are not the only people who die of sin, and educated villains and talented rogues do the most mischief. Men who have walked the earth masterpieces of vice have climbed the heights of Parnassus and charmed the world with their art, music, and poesy. We claim, however, that the tendency of an awakened, educated mind, unless in vicious environment, is to higher reason. The crystal gate to the palace of all that is good and beautiful is close by when a man stops to think. The great trouble is that many do not think. They are down in the realm of sense, feed on society, read novels, dream, sleep, and do not think, except about something good to eat or pretty to wear. They start in school, start many things, but they are fickle because thoughtless. They are flirts; flirt with their own fortunes, flirt with their friends, flirt with the truth, flirt with their own souls, flirt with God. Some get an ugly twist in their brains, like that in a gnarled oak, and everything goes into the twist. They twist the truth, twist the stars, twist life to fit the grain of their

79

bad bump of pride; cranks cannot think. Give me a thinker, even if he doubts; I would rather risk one with brains out in this awful whirlpool.

Education is not only not easy, it is slow. The growth of mind is slow. It is not a holiday trip; it cannot be done by the job. Murat bored eight years for living water at Grenville. Virgil lived ten years with his shadowy heroes of the Æneid. Field was thirteen years putting his cable under the ocean. It took one hundred and fifty years to lift the dome of St. Peter's and but a few months to build the White City at Chicago; the one is a real university, the other a summer school—where they give degrees. So many sneer at the long years of a college course and its cost. They pile up the names of great men who never saw a college. Yes, in spite of the disadvantage, by the greatness of their genius, and even more by the heroic efforts to compensate their conscious lack, they succeeded. They took Greek and Latin on horseback, grammar in the barracks, like Cobbett, the English statesman, who said: "My knapsack was my bookcase"; astronomy like Rittenhouse, his diagrams on his plough handles; law like Abraham Lincoln, by the light of his kitchen fire; or philosophy like Burke, reading Locke on the Understanding in a tallow-chandler's shop. And think you that a thorough course in college would have been injurious to them? Did West Point hinder the genius of Grant, or Annapolis that of Dewey, or Oxford that of John Wesley? Did Yale and Harvard cramp the writers of the Constitution, or chill the courage of the signers of the Declaration of Independence, or the patriotism of its sons who fought at the Battle of Lexington?

With or without the college training, education is a life work. Stephenson studied, toiled, and agonized fifteen years at his locomotive; Watt thirty years on his engine. How long did it take to coin the jewels of art, literature, and science? How long to prepare that reply to the argument of Hayne in the Senate? How long, how long to make Daniel Webster? How many years and how much study in such a giant as William E. Gladstone? "It took thirty years," said the sculptor, "to make that bust in ten days." Michael Angelo created the device of an old man in a go-cart with an hour-glass, bearing the motto, "Ancor imparo"—*I am still learning.*

Begun in pain and adversity, there is ultimate joy which is not easily counterfeited or surpassed. The Universe is full of suggestion and tongues. Nature to the open mind never is exhausted; in age it is made more glowing and eloquent by all the seasons past. The birds of each spring are sweeter in their warble, the flowers have a richer perfume and beauty, for the memory of all the years in them. It puts man *en rapport* with the science, literature, and poesy of the ages. No matter what his company, or who his neighbors, or what skies overhead, he can walk with the heroes and live in all ages in the great home of history, walk with the old philosophers of the Academy, visit with the sages of old Greece, and travel in all lands.

Elect souls in garrets outwitting hunger until the skin clung to their bones because they heard the throbbing of the engines, the rattle of the wheels, the noise of wings, saw the lightnings, the sailing of ships, landscapes of beauty, angels in marble, are in an apocalypse as much alone as John on Patmos. You need not pity them, they could starve on such visions, and the very contagion feeds loving hearts about them, toiling as did old Palissy among his pottery with hungry eyes watching his experiments. They could sit in dungeons and think out "Delectable Mountains." Without fire they could turn to ashes, in public opinion, and no more than old Ridley covet another's crown. Is there any herald prophet who can foretell such things?

Go fathom the bliss of Columbus when he saw that shore lifting out of the ocean, or when he kissed the soil of San Salvador. Measure their joy when the lightnings were yet playing only in the thoughts of Morse and Franklin; the iron horse thundering only in the brain of Stephenson, or the steamship yet afloat in the soul of Fulton, or astronomy yet rising in the mental dome of Newton and Copernicus; there where the grand thought is fledging into the angel, it cannot be painted by any Raphael.

EDUCATION AND CHARACTER

Ignorance carries its own retribution. It is not bliss. In its tortuous mistakes it is a blind serpent, often striking friends and foes alike. In its dregs are chagrin and regret; it may rave and riot, raise its red flag and enroll its anarchists and issue the fiats of a mob, but they file off one by one each with his own shame. The devil makes just dividends. There is no fraud in the wages. Satan's servant must face his own blushes. Like Milo, alone in the forest, his fingers caught in the rebounding oak, he is a victim of his own stupidity.

Many want the honor or power of education, but are not willing to pay its cost, and it's a cheap article you get in any market for nothing.

There are some things a man may have and excite no envy. He may be meek as Moses, as patient as Job, and walk the streets of Egypt, Uz, and Sodom, and nobody envy him. They may want the rod which could cut the sea open or coax water from a rock, but not the meekness of Moses. They may want the sheep and camels of Job, but envy him for his piety little more than for his boils. There is no envious crowd hanging about a man's closet; you can't get a corner in a prayer-meeting. People will crowd the cars and pay full fare for only a sight of greatness they can never reach, but there is no rush on the road by way of the college to God's everlasting honors.

Do not forget that you have too much in you for a

cheap, worldly life, too much for the stings of a fashionable calling; you are too great to be a plaything for society, a figurehead for its frivolities; too much of an eagle to be a stool pigeon for any such designs.

In this progress you will more and more feel that there are almost unused functions in your soul. If one has a genius for art or music or language or invention which has lain dormant by reason of ignorance or has been smothered by some other calling, there will be times when it will stir. In the presence of some masterpiece of art, under the power of exquisite melody, or before some ingenious mechanism will not the mind catch fire, strange music start up in the soul, visions of beauty rise in the brain and plead for canvas and colors?

So are there not already signs not only of intellectual, but also of spiritual powers, as yet slightly touched with dormant pictures of rest, uneasy miracles of motion of which you are capable, vastly beyond anything you have yet known in the wildest flush of other triumphs? Are there not evidences that you have links in you of bliss or woe which have never been payed out, music in you beyond Beethoven symphonies, power to climb above the vulture's flight on the glowing mountains which Bunyan saw through the grates of the Bedford jail, strength to go where even the stars are only torches to show the way up to the gates of God's great City? Without this consciousness, how little of a man! Be as God meant you, especially since the evolutionists claim that it is only in spirit and spirit life that man essentially differs from his brute progenitor. Then, with his higher ideal and life, whatever experiences in the ups or downs, through defiles or deep cañons, you may be sure you are ever *en route* to those white summits of which you may have had now and then some glimpses.

VI

THE TEST OF THE BABE
A CHRISTMAS SERMON

"And Simeon blessed them, and said unto Mary his mother, Behold, this child is set for the fall and rising again of many in Israel; and for a sign which shall be spoken against."

LUKE ii. 34.

THE Babe of Bethlehem, as many another, found this an inhospitable world. There was no room for Him in the inn. He who came to open heaven to the outcast race had no place but a stable where He could be born. His first night on earth He slept on straw with the beasts of burden.

His reception here was in wide contrast with the ado that night in the skies above His lowly birthplace. Were not those bright Beings, who set the heavens afire as they came through, pulsing with the "Glad tidings of great joy to all people," surprised that the world was not up and astir? One of them had to go all the way down to the only people he could find awake, and tell them in so many words, "Unto you is born this day, in the city of David, a Saviour which is Christ the Lord. Ye shall find the Babe wrapped in swaddling clothes and lying in a manger."

If the fulness of time had come, if the voices of all the prophets were converging to a point, if the object-teaching of the ages by the law had fitted the minds of His people and they were "waiting for the consolation of Israel," why did not the very air, tremulous with the great expectation, break forth in melodious response: "Glory to God in the highest"? With the exception of some elect souls that announcement was met with an ominous silence. No wonder the angels soon went back into heaven. Perhaps, if they were not in the secret, they went back from the cold world in silence.

The story of that night must have been told the next day in Jerusalem, discussed on the streets and about the Temple and in every Jewish home. It was soon blazed from Gaza to Tyre; the fishermen of Capernaum must have talked about it as they cast their nets in Galilee; the politicians in Jericho, and the Scribes in the Holy City began to search again the old scrolls, and ears were turned to the skies every night; it was being hushed up, when lo, God lights a star for some eyes outside of Israel.

From the East, perhaps from Persia, the wise men come inquiring for Him whose star they have seen. These newcomers confirm the story of the shepherds.

THE TEST OF THE BABE

King Herod is in trouble! All Jerusalem is wild with excitement! Herod hurries the religious teachers together and demands where Christ is to be born, and they tell him forever, they can never take it back, "In Bethlehem of Judæa."

Now the wise men hurry on the six miles to Bethlehem to do homage to the Wonderful Babe and return to their country. Then the bloody episode of Herod's slaughter of the innocents and, with the pitiful voice of Ramah, the stories and stir about the new-born Messiah appear to die away. Do the crowd believe that Herod has killed the Messiah? Do the Sanhedrim also strangely stop all investigation because they think the Hope of Israel has been slain?

Things seem to drift on quietly until the silence is broken by that "voice in the wilderness of Judæa," startling the slumbering masses, "Repent ye, for the Kingdom of Heaven is at hand."

But there were some, we know not how many, who saw all these things with different eyes. When the mother of John broke out with the spirit of prophecy; when Mary by the same inspiration responded, "My soul doth magnify the Lord," and the dumb Zacharias began to praise God, it is said, "And fear came on all that dwelt round about them, and all these sayings were noised abroad throughout all the hill country of Judæa"; and all they that heard them laid them up in their hearts. And what wonderful things came from the loosed tongue of Zacharias!

So, too, when Joseph and Mary brought the Babe into the Temple, there stood a man who was strangely watching for them. He took the child into his arms and said, "Mine eyes have seen Thy salvation!" Then too, a woman eighty-four years old, who lived in the Temple, "coming in at that instant, gave thanks likewise unto the Lord and spake of him to all them that looked for redemption in Jerusalem." We know not how many more there were who saw the nature of this wonderful Babe.

It is always so. It is so to-day. Simeon, who knew Him, said this strange thing of Him: "Behold, this child is set for the fall and rising again of many in Israel; and for a sign which shall be spoken against; that the thoughts of many hearts may be revealed." This solemn fact is verified by all the ages since He was born. Human souls come to a crisis when they touch Him. See yonder in that thoroughfare a stone over which all feet must pass. Some feet strike it and stumble, and thenceforth in life choose to stumble on and down amid blindness of thought and scenes of sin and ever-deepening shadows; others touch it and are thrilled with a new life; the eye sparkles, the face beams with smiles, it is a step up into another pathway over whose terminus are breaking clouded pictures of joy. This wonderful Babe is declared by Isaiah, eight hundred years before Simeon, to be this magnetic stone. "A rock of offence," he says, "a stone of stumbling, set for the rise or fall of many in Israel."

He who can look into the face of any baby as it looks up into his eyes with a smile, as if to challenge his caress, its innocence a voice out of his own blessed past, its helplessness a prayer to his strength, and meet it with a scowl of hate, or a rude blow for its smile, not only evinces the intrinsic badness of his nature, but in that instant of hate or ugliness goes down a notch lower in his own wretched soul and destiny. No one can give a baby a smile without getting a tiny sign of light to lift him a little higher. But to-day in this other Babe is wrapped the whole life and character and mission of the Son of God; and whenever He comes into the distant view of the soul with a challenge for its homage then is the test.

The method of His announcement is a test of sincerity. The star brought the Magi perhaps a thousand miles. The great Jewish Sanhedrim, who were so troubled at the testimony of the Magi, would not go six miles to ascertain whether the glorious rumors were founded in fact. If they had taken pains to investigate in the real spirit of inquiry, they ought to have seen as much in the Babe as did the old woman of the Temple. But no, these rumors were not in line with their preconceived theory of the coming of Christ. "Surely God would have shown it to the Sanhedrim! The idea, that He would make a star for these foreigners! Bring these Gentile astrologers to tell us of the birth of the King of the Jews! That He would send angels to sing at midnight to those ignorant shepherds! It must have been the Northern Lights they saw, and voices of song which they heard floating on the still air at night from Jerusalem!" And so in their pride they dismissed it all. The others thought as their teachers did, and did not believe enough to go to Bethlehem.

God did not send any more angels; He did not light any more stars, and so "He came unto His own and His own received Him not;" and with such a start in unbelief they were blind enough to face all the noon of Christ's miracles and manifestation of God; they knew Him not, but crucified the Lord of glory.

So it is forever. To the lowly spirit of real inquiry Christ evinces Himself until every doubt is swallowed up in His out-beaming divinity.

Think of the Christmas of our childhood. The scenery is all changed; the star, the Magi, the shepherds with their flocks, the angels, the stable of the inn and the Babe in the manger, all so changed. No, they have not changed, but we have. The world about us is different; our friends, our home, our prospects. We look through different eyes, we have had so much experience. The

THE TEST OF THE BABE

long range shows the greater contrast, but often the changes are swift, and really none of us come to the same Christmas we had a year ago. We are sadder or merrier on a holiday, nearer to the Christ Child, or colder and farther away. We do not see this Babe in the lowly cradle as we did then. Some of us see more in Him, some of us less; some may look at Him through tears, some through neglected duty, through settled shadows of doubt, and the view is distant and cold; to some the vivid vision of Christ is faded until it is like that dying portrait on the wall; but there are devout souls whose clear eyes see enough in their Saviour to-day to outwit the very sting of death; every glance gets a new sunbeam; every look a face full of holy light and a gaze gets a full-orbed Deity; there are those who see like Simeon; some who have gotten beyond stars and angels away amid the burning depths of the "Invisible."

Of all the sermons to-day, no two will be alike, if the preacher speaks out of his own present visions of this Babe. Some will speak better things of Him, but there will be men who will be able to say worse things about Christ than ever, because their minds are darker and they have more hate; they will preach of the Babe, of course, to-day because it is the fashion; they will give gifts to-morrow to their friends for the same reason; they will go to His cradle and, like Herod, talk of His divinity with daggers in their hands. There never was a time when Christ was hated so terribly as He is to-day. He will be hated more and more as He shines on. He will be adored more as the world moves on in Christian intelligence, as He rises like His star in the heavens.

He is a moral test in the manner of His coming. I need not stop to picture the style with which the world would have clothed His coming. If only word had been sent to the world that the Son of God was to be born, it would have beaten Nero's *Aurora Domus* in a palace for Him; it would have swaddled Him as a prince; it would have jewelled His cradle; it would have made every mountain of Palestine blaze; sent silver-voiced heralds to every shore and rivalled the angels with its music. But its pride was mortally hurt by the mode of Christ's coming. Was ever royal blood cradled so lowly? Did any other crowned head start on such a pillow? How can this proud world ever forgive the fashion of Jesus' birth? It never has forgiven Him. It has hated the Babe, as it has many another baby, for being born so lowly. How it has tried to rescue Him by the genius of art; how it has tried to make men forget His cradle by setting His religion on thrones, making it gorgeous and fantastic and æsthetic!

No, this worldly spirit shrinks from the test of the manger. That lowly birthplace is harder to decorate and transfigure to suit human pride than the cross itself, for it seems that God had more to do with His birth; the cross was a work of art; God put His cradle beside that of the lowest that no one might feel "He is above me"; the Father meant Him a Saviour of the lowest; and this real spirit of inquiry accepts Him where He is and as He is, puts its pride in the dust, and is willing, whatever the station or estate, to be rocked as lowly as its Lord, and so is able to enter into His rest.

God saw that no ingenuity of art or magnificence in religion can fill a proud heart; no jewelled bowl of incense waft off its sorrow. I appeal to all history for facts, that the worthiest heads for crowns of all sorts, the brains which have thought deepest into the secrets of the Creator, thought out the truest beauty and the noblest devices next to the motions of nature, and soared highest in all skies, and the hearts, too, which have dwelt apart in peace and drank the deepest of joys older than the world, have been those consenting to take them all, both the ideas and the joys of God, on the level with the manger. So God wasted His best music on the shepherds and put His own Son in the cradle of an outcast. So the Babe is a rock of offence, a stone of stumbling to the proud.

Thus Christ in the mode of His kingdom is a test. It was crosswise of the spirit of the world. Think of starting the conquest of this world with a voice, a voice crying in the wilderness of Judæa, a voice with no bayonet back of it! A preacher, the truth, the Spirit! Pray tell

me how much the worldly spirit respects such a warrior.
Go to Transvaal and try it. Why, every drop of our
blood by nature has a fist in it, a declaration of war.
The only difference between savage and civilized blood
is, one has a tomahawk and the other a needle-gun in it.
Every bit of the carnal mind is militant; it is uneasy out
of uniform; it worships the soldier; it shows its scars
and gloats over its scenes of blood. So it is all through
the earth yet, the halo of glory encircles the brow of the
warrior; victory by force of arms is glory! A throne
without a standing army under it is yet a plaything in this
savage world. No wonder, then, that the people who had
been trodden down and crushed until there was peace
wanted a soldier for a Saviour. No wonder they wanted
a warrior so much—believed in him so much. Force!
blood! Those were the only things their enemies would
respect. Oh, how they wanted to fight; how they ached
for a divine general! They would have dared the eagle
and followed him, wading in blood, to Rome.

So yet, the spirit of fight is in our veins; we see wrong
and meanness and lawlessness and high-handed sin and
the blind instincts of our savage nature feel for the war-
club. It is easier to start a crusade. You can get up a
larger insurrection than a prayer-meeting; men will go
farther to see a fight than a revival. So, too, when an
insult stings in the sensitive soul it wakes up the savage.
Wherever there is the black head of calumny or treason,

like Peter, man reaches for the sword. But see there, old Herod, Israel! look, ye savage, bloody spirit of the world! it is a Babe in the manger, not a warrior; it is the Prince of Peace! "He shall not strive nor cry nor lift up His voice in the streets."

Hark! Yonder He sits on the Mount: "Blessed are the peace-makers"; "Blessed are the meek"; "Love them that hate you." See Him yonder on Calvary. Hark! "Forgive them for they know not what they do." Look! He is going away, rising up into the heavens, and His last message floats down through the ages, "Go ye into all the world and preach the gospel to every creature."

Whatever may be the dire necessities forced on us in self-defence by war, it is certain if any human heart is ever conquered, any hate, any sin, it must be by the method of Jesus Christ. You cannot hate a man down or cure his hostility by revenge; you must conquer by the spirit of truth and the love of Christ. It is the Babe, not the warrior. The spirit of the world says the survival of the fittest; the principle of the Babe says the survival of the weakest, for when I am weak then am I strong.

Then, the next strongest passion to war and conquest is that of parade, the power of parade, the love of it. It is in us to fling out banners; to be seen of men; to make a noise and a show. "Eyes and Ears." Read history and see how men have tried to make the religion of Jesus showy; and in just so much they have hidden its power and made it weak in the hearts of men. The showy tends to the artificial. The strongest forces in this world are the most silent; the weakest often make the most noise and show. Is it that we believe that men are really overcome, sin overcome, by a parade of wealth and greatness? It would have been our way to set the heavens ablaze and sky-rocket every miracle. We would have had that scene at Bethlehem and chorus of angels in sight and hearing of Jerusalem; had it rehearsed every Christmas. But you cannot convert the world by theatres, even with angels for actors and stars for footlights. Dead souls cannot be waked to real visions of Christ by any ecclesiastical mimicry. So He who began in a manger did not lift up His voice in the street; He sent astonished men, who had felt His miraculous power, away with, "See thou tell no man." There was in His holy, sensitive nature a shrinking from the gaze of men. Christ hated ostentation. He might have had a chariot and ridden over Jerusalem in state; He might have had, He said, twelve legions of angels—He went about afoot. It was simplicity, nothing for show. He never looked for astonishment, never waited for applause. It was the sweet simplicity of the Babe through His whole life, and so is a divine test to every heart. It is enough that the disciple be as his Lord. Do men forget that the good things they do in secret for the Master have tongues of their own and do not need to be published? He who cannot wait until eternity for such fame is unworthy of it. He who prays, like the Pharisee, to be heard of men, Christ says, gets his pay down and is the cheapest hand in the market. Forgive me, if I say I would not give a cent a million for such prayers and other like goods in proportion. It is he who consents to be gauged by the manger, to walk on the same level and in the shadow of his Lord who feels in his soul the secret and the sources of his Lord's power. That is the power of the Babe.

Finally, the holiness is the crucial test. He drew some souls to Him like a magnet; others flew off in hate. You smile back again and love that baby because it is a picture of innocence. I said it is a tiny sign to your moral estate. If your heart answers to this final test and clings to the person of Christ who is not only the image of all which is beautiful and true and holy, but the personality of holiness and the image of the invisible, must there not come to your soul a secret sign better than a visible star to assure your heart and make it merry as those of the Magi when they saw that light over Bethlehem on their way to the Saviour? If you do not love Him, if your heart draws back from the holy, beautiful Christ, is it not the polarity of sin? Is it not ominous as that starless, songless sky under which so many walked after the first Christmas?

How much, then, do we see and feel as we come to the

manger? how much of the fulness which dwelt in Him? He will show Himself as we are able to appreciate Him. He would, perhaps, have taken all the disciples to His transfiguration had they been up to it. Only three had seen enough of Him to be qualified for this unfolding; but John had to be in Patmos many years before he could see the apocalypse. In it he saw a wonder in heaven: a woman clothed with the sun, under her feet the moon and on her head a crown of stars; with her a babe, a man-child, which was caught up to the throne of God, and over the shining lights came floating down the strains of a wonderful song, "Now is come salvation and the kingdom of our God and the power of His Christ." The child of the manger cradled in the sun and caught up to the throne of God!

Must God put us in some Patmos, some Bedford jail, some eclipse of the world, so that we may hear such music, see the glory and believe in the ultimate triumph of Christ?

This Babe is standing in the sun. Behold Him! He will yet mount the throne of God.

VII

IMMORTALITY IN THE OLD
TESTAMENT

"HOMER sang of what he saw," said Ruskin, "Phidias carved what he saw, Raphael painted the men of his own time in their own caps and mantles. Truth to nature," he argues, "is the true genius of all art."

Doubtless no one of us has looked at first upon the frescos and copies or originals of even the masters without a feeling of disappointment and without thinking there is too much color and art and too little nature. They all seem but glorious caricatures, gorgeous, but fictitious, and we do not wonder that the great reformers banished them from the Christian temples, perhaps more for this than for any other reason, that a sense of their unreality and dreamy idealism is transferred to the living scenes of the Bible, making them distant and unreal. Moses, Elijah, David, and Isaiah, in their paintings, are heroic and Homeric rather than the real flesh and blood of those old men of God. And still more do we revolt from the painted Christ and the apostles and the awful travesties of gospel scenes. All this results partly from a fashion of art, which has changed like the fashions of dress, but mostly from the forcing of these sacred characters and events to the peculiar plot or ideal of the artist's brain.

Now just such havoc has often been made of these same realities by the subjective methods of what is called criticism. By every art known to subtle and suggestive doubt, the sceptics have sought to turn into poetry and parable the mighty verities of distant history. There are so-called Christian temples which are frescoed with these mythical caricatures of significant facts. The purpose of this vandalism is easily understood: they wish to deplete the history of miracle; they would strip Mount Sinai of its lightnings; they would make the story of creation a vision; would shake down this lifted curtain of Revelation, and give us only their painted pictures upon it, instead of the great living landscapes, with real men and things, and a real God among them. And then, too, with no real sky, no heaven above the head of patriarch or prophet, they would make Mount Zion as dark as Olympus and Moses no more inspired than Confucius. In their passionate zeal, they rub out all the light and miraculous element possible. True, there have been many who do not feel that there is much light in all the Old Testament on the future life, or that it is at all a vital question; who believe that it is not essential to either the character or accountability of the Hebrews. Others feel that their own faith is bound up in the question whether the Old Testament really taught immortality.

Now, it is not claimed that there is no obscurity, that it is all light. As far as absolute, direct teaching is concerned, life and immortality are only brought to light in clear, bold relief in the Gospel. The sun has risen, but there were stars in that sky over Israel.

The question starts, Why did not Moses clearly unfold immortality and put the sanctions of eternity upon the decalogue? There are many possible reasons, though God's ways are not our ways.

The doctrine may have been so well understood that all this was implied. Certainly it was a part of the religious faith of Egypt, where the children of Israel had lived four hundred years. It was, indeed, in the faith of all nations and is interwoven with all their traditions and mythology.

This code of laws was not a system of theology any more than is any other code, and these fugitive slaves were sunken into a moral state which required immediate rewards and penalties. There must be something definite and tangible and close by to be efficient. They must be coaxed with milk and honey and have arrows drunk with blood to spur them to any decent life or to a spot where they could appreciate anything higher. They, too, had had a bitter experience in the house of their bondage with those who professed to believe in the retributions of eternity, so that possibly it was purposely kept aloof from this system of government and yet firmly fixed in their belief.

They were too fresh from the gorgeous idolatry of Egypt, and the great idea to be made emphatic was the being and unity of God, which alone is the source and sanction of all government.

It was a theocracy. The personal, great "I am" was their king, and the awful signs on Mount Sinai, in the tabernacle and in the burning cloud, of His immediate presence as Lawgiver, Executor, and Saviour were enough. There was so much of God that it met all cavil and all faith, even if it did not imply and assure immortality.

Is that not still the truth? He who becomes conscious of God in a divine experience finds an end of doubt and does not need specific solutions of any trouble. The child who was found in some dread place clings to his father's hand, looks up into his face and goes on, even through rough and dark passages, without fear of the result. He may prattle on the way, and when the feet are tired curiously ask questions: "Where is it you are leading me, my father? How long is the way?" but he doubts no more than the sheep doubt the shepherd whose word they hear on the way to green pastures, or Lazarus doubts the fair beings who are lifting him to realms of light. It seems to me that the vividness and miraculous nearness of God would drown all questions and assure any thoughtful slave in that caravan.

Then it appears, too, that everything about their history was significant of another life. How cheap and flat the whole enterprise of a peculiar people! The commonwealth of Israel! What a farce the Exodus! What an awful grandeur for nothing the giving of the law, the bloody ritual for an atonement for sin or an idea of holiness! The very land of promise and the dispossessing of the Canaanites and the war of conquest, if it all terminated in "That your days may be long in the land that the Lord your God giveth you," and had no reference, as a world object-lesson, to the long days of another life! Their great leader, at least, "endured not only as seeing Him that is invisible," but had "respect unto the recompense of reward." This surely was not merely a house and lot in the land of Canaan. If so, for his pains, he only had a glimpse of it before he died, from a distant mountain top, and suffered a great disappointment.

The Sadducees, the materialists, who denied the existence of angel or spirit, the soul separate from the body, as well as the resurrection and any future life, came to our Lord with their stupid puzzle. The reply was, "Ye do err, not knowing the Scriptures or the power of God;" the Scriptures which teach the existence of the soul and the life to come and the power which is able to raise the dead. Did not God say to Moses out of the burning bush, "I am the God of Abraham and of Isaac and of Jacob;" "God is not the God of the dead, but of the living"? Did Moses err, with the Sadducees, or did he know all that awful voice implied? These old Scriptures, then, did teach the doctrine of living after death, and even the burning bush on distant Horeb is a beacon to the gates of everlasting life. Possibly the Saviour took the most occult fact to meet their blind cavil and to show them their want of spiritual insight—the condition which shuts men out of the deeper revelations of the Scriptures. If they had taken the same pains to find the light in God's word which they had taken to obscure it and to put out their faith, they would have found enough to show their souls into the great blessed relief.

God does not cram His revelations down unwilling throats. There must be an anxious attitude toward the truth and a spirit dilated, like an eye in the night. Then God's lights begin to shine into it like the stars. So he who shuts his eyes under this sky of the old dispensation or any other, will find it easy to see only a black vault, even if God should tear open the heavens.

But said Dives, "Send back a man from the dead and they will believe." Believe what? That there is another life and retribution! Teach them the truth about this other world. "Nay, if they believe not Moses and the prophets, neither will they repent though one rose from the dead." Moses and the prophets did, then, teach and were understood by the Jews as teaching, something more than retribution on earth, if Jesus, who put the word into the mouth of Abraham, was not mistaken.

Then again, Paul said that Abraham "By faith sojourned in the land of promise as in a strange country, dwelling in tabernacles, with Isaac and Jacob, the heirs with him of the same promise, for he looked for a city which hath foundations, whose builder and maker is God." How believe in a city? Did he think that God was going to build a tangible city on Mount Zion? Was he waiting around in Hebron in his tent expecting to see the stones and trees roll up into a great city, built without hands? Did he go out in the morning and look to see a city gorgeous and glittering in the rising sun? Or watch to see it come bodily out of the skies? O, no, "These all died in the faith . . . but now they desire a better country; that is, an heavenly;" country, city, and all; "wherefore God is not ashamed to be called their God, for He hath prepared for them a city." If we believe the inspired author of the Hebrews, Abraham looked for a city which was not on earth, but in heaven. Could he hold such a glorious faith and not teach it to Isaac and Isaac to Jacob? Could such a faith die out? Nay, "All these," away back to Abel, "died in the faith." And did not Moses understand this? And then, when he wrote his story of Abram, he said that God told Abram, "Fear not, I am

thy shield and thy exceeding great reward." Not merely
a few acres of land, more or less, over in Palestine; it
was this, beyond all such poor estate: "I, thy Creator,
I am thy exceeding great reward." How long, Moses,
did you intend to say that the infinite and everlasting
"I Am" would be the reward of Abraham? How long
did Abraham expect it? How long would any man, not
an incorrigible sceptic, understand by that? Just while
he was wandering about in Canaan with his tent, his
sheep, and camels? And then, just when he had come to
know and appreciate the friendship and beauty and glory
of the ever-living and ever-blessed God, bury him in the
same grave with his camel and that the end of it? Did
Abraham ever think so? Or Moses? That God could
tell him, "I am thy exceeding great reward," thrilling
every fibre of his being with such a consciousness of Him
that he could endure the supreme test and deliberately
go to Mount Moriah to offer his only son Isaac, the child
of promise, and all the time thinking that to-morrow the
"great reward" would slip from his cold fingers with all
earth's poor possessions and God's friendship perish
forever? What an ineffable mockery such a friendship and "reward"! No, under such a faith Abraham
would have gone to Moriah for suicide rather than for
sacrifice!

Hark, down the ages farther, you hear the sweet notes
of a harp and see a lifted face filled with light and possi-

bly a tear on the cheek. "The Lord is the portion of mine inheritance." How long, David? Why, "My flesh and my heart faileth, but God is the strength of my heart and my portion forever." "To eternity," is the Hebrew. They can wring nothing else out of these words but a great hope of eternal life.

That old promise is another star above the tent of Mamre in the sky of the Old Testament, and the sceptics cannot put it out.

Then, too, here are strange signs of another life and estate. Suppose our memory of this world's geography were blotted out and we had nothing but our conjectures that there was any other continent; the cable had been cut and the ships sunken. If, all at once, a man should appear among us of such peculiar dress, features, and speech that we were sure he was a foreigner; whatever his business, or however he came, his very being would confirm our conjectures—there must be another country. Now these records say that there have been some distinguished foreigners on these shores.

See yonder, approaching the old tent under the oaks of Mamre, where sits this same great patriarch, those mysterious strangers. Abraham recognizes them in spite of their disguises and entertains accordingly. They were on their way to Sodom. Another such visitor, with a drawn sword in his hand, met Joshua at Jericho, and in deference to him Joshua took the shoes from his feet.

Another stood in the path of the old prophet of Moab. One, in the guise of a wayfarer with a staff in his hand, sat under an oak in Ophrah as Gideon was threshing by the wine-press. One came in a great crisis in Israel. He proved what he was by drawing fire out of the rock with the staff in his hand. "But this was the angel of the covenant," you say. Still it does not hurt the force of the argument. Now, did not the coming of these mysterious foreigners prove to them and us and teach all the world that there was, at least, a supernatural estate out of which they came, if not, indeed, another world, a celestial world, somewhere? If you could by the cold acids of doubt dissolve these bright beings into myths or visions, still they would stand out there in this Testament, like the vision of Jacob at Peniel, showing and teaching to their faith at least, if not to ours, the mighty fact of such an estate.

This record also shows that this estate and world were meant for immortal man as well as angels; that there was a way up as well as down, and that the golden gate swings both ways.

Moses writes the story of a man and his glorious taking off, which ought to settle the question. "And Enoch walked with God: and he was not; for God took him;" just put His everlasting arm around him and lifted him out of the world. You may say that is only a quiet way of announcing his death; but he says that Adam died and Seth died and Kenan died and Mahalaleel died and Jared,

the father of Enoch, died, and then "Enoch was not, for
God took him." Then did the author of Hebrews tell
the truth—"By faith Enoch was translated that he should
not see death." What object teaching of immortality
was this, in this great word-picture of Moses? Back in
the early days of the race a man three hundred and sixty-
five years old, who lived with God, a holy walking pro-
test against the growing wickedness of the times, one
day after his work is done and his feet slow with years
"was not." They looked for him everywhere, but
could get no trace of him. They had no funeral for
Enoch. Moses said "God took him." Took him where?
Smuggled him off into annihilation, or chloroformed him
to sleep until the resurrection? No, God kidnapped
Enoch for a better purpose. He "was translated." Was
it a whirlwind or a gust of joy which carried him off?
Surely he had a good excuse for leaving as he did. God
called, and he hurried away without giving the world
notice, and before it missed him he was beyond its hate
and death's venomed arrow, passing somewhere on his
way in the twinkling of an eye that change which awaits
those who remain at the coming of the Lord, and staring
angels stood back to let him through the gates. Did
Moses teach a future life? He believed it so much he
did not stop to argue or assert; he simply told this as a
matter of course, which all would understand: "He was
not, for God took him." A man walking off the earth

into the heavens! The translated Enoch is another star in that old sky.

True, there are many passages through the Old Testament, especially in Job, which seem to imply doubt and despair, as if the grave is the end of man. And yet a little study of them shows that mainly they imply the end of man here; just as we speak of death and the grave; as far as life and beauty and joy of the world, this is the end of them. Such texts as these: "As the cloud is consumed and vanisheth away so he that goeth down to the grave shall come up no more." If we stop there it seems the end, but the next verse shows it refers to this life: "He shall return no more to his house, neither shall his place know him any more." And the Psalmist says, as a plea for present mercy, "For in death there is no remembrance of Thee; in the grave who shall give Thee thanks?" Again, "Shall the dust praise Thee?" Isaiah mourns, "For the grave cannot praise Thee; death cannot celebrate Thee; they that go down into the pit cannot hope for Thy truth; the living, the living shall praise Thee as I do this day." This is just as we speak of the dead. "They know not anything; their sons come to honor and they know it not." "They are done with this world, its modes of life and thought and its opportunities." These say nothing of what is beyond the grave; these are only like our elegies over the dead, only our "Earth to earth and dust to dust"; but out of the very dust of even those old graves rises a bird to sing of life. "Who knoweth the spirit of man which goeth upward and the spirit of the beast which goeth downward to the earth?" Then says the same preacher at the last, after all the vanities when the "silver cord is loosed and the golden bowl broken," "Then shall the dust return to the earth as it was: and the spirit shall return unto God who gave it." "The wicked," he says, "is driven away in his wickedness; but the righteous hath hope in his death." What a strange time to hope! He says many sad things of human life and its disappointments in words of sackcloth and sprinkled with ashes, which just fit millions of poor, aching hearts, and are at home in this world always. Of these words he is not anxious to keep a record; he just pours out his cries on the throbbing air, to die or drift on the winds, but now, as if a spirit hand has passed across his eyes, as if an ecstasy has dropped on him, he sees something worth writing down: "Oh, that my words were now written; oh, that they were printed in a book." Nay, a book is too transient, and he calls for a pen of iron to grave them "in a rock forever." What is it, Job, you would write? And he says, "For I know that my redeemer liveth, and that He shall stand at the latter day upon the earth: and though after my skin worms destroy this body, yet in my flesh shall I see God." Whether his tired, smitten soul just then fell back on his mighty faith, or whether a miraculous vision of his Redeemer stood out as in the Apocalypse, we know not. From above the hills of Galilee, as if he saw over the gulf of the last sorrow a section of this bright promise of God, through a coming Saviour; for this bow, made upon the tears of death by this Son of the world, starts from Eden's gate and dips in the ocean beyond time's last shore. And, cries the Psalmist, "Thou shalt guide me with Thy counsel and afterward receive me to glory." Did he mean a dreamless grave? Was this the glory which shone in his eye as he gazed into the shadows of the valley? "My flesh also shall rest in hope, for Thou wilt not leave my soul in Sheol," which, even as prophetic of Christ's resurrection, includes his personal hope and "Thou wilt show me the path of life," a way out into life; "in Thy presence is fulness of joy and at Thy right hand there are pleasures forever more." Did David teach eternal life? He prays, "Deliver my soul from men who have their portion in this life. . . As for me, I will behold Thy face in righteousness; I will be satisfied, when I awake, with Thy likeness." Whether he meant from the grave in the resurrection, or the sleep of death in a glorious eternity, it is the same mighty hope of immortality. There is death in the palace. The baby is white and cold; and death, in a coffin of gold, is death. The royal father has spent seven days and nights fasting and crying to God; he lay all night on the ground and remorse was mixed with his tears; he knew that his child was suffering for his sin and his heart was aching with a double sorrow; but now it is over and the forgiven penitent looks into the pale, waxen face of his darling and says, "I shall go to him, but he shall not return to me." Go to him in the mildew of the grave? Was that his mighty hope? Was he wringing comfort out of the ashes of death for that hour, that one day he should lie down beside his dead baby in the tomb? O, no! Did he not see through his tears the bright spirit-child living in the fair scenes of Paradise, as he cried "I shall go to him"? How has the world understood David? Tell me, you who have cradled your children in the grave! How often has it been said to the mourner? Your mother's heart beats the cold exegesis of the sceptic and feels the pulse and vision of David's great hope.

Have you ever read that vision of Daniel by the great river, where He whose form was as beryl, whose face was as lightning, and His eyes as lamps of fire, touched him from his swoon and gave him strength to hear of the last days? "When many of them that sleep in the dust shall awake, some to everlasting life, some to everlasting shame and contempt, and they that be wise shall shine as the brightness of the firmament, and they that turn many to righteousness as the stars forever and ever." No matter when or how, in this grand old prophecy of

Daniel there breaks through the shadows of death an everlasting life and a vision of souls burning as the stars in our sky "forever and ever."

And Malachi, the last of the old prophets said, "Then they that feared the Lord spake often one to another: and the Lord hearkened and heard it, and a book of remembrance was written before Him for them that feared the Lord and that thought upon His name. And they shall be mine, saith the Lord of hosts, in that day when I make up my jewels." What day? They soon were dead; their bones were laid beside the scoffers; but Malachi says a day is coming when God shall show His jewels, holy immortal spirits who clung to His promises in bad times and went to sleep looking for the Messiah. Ah, the eye of the old prophet sparkles as he points his finger. "Jewels yonder glittering through the mists of death."

"Thy dead men shall live," shouts Isaiah, back there three hundred years before, "the earth also shall disclose her blood, and shall no more cover her slain." "Awake and sing, ye that dwell in the dust," and so he, too, preaches the gospel of the resurrection, which is also the gospel of immortality.

Whatever the mystery or shadows which gathered over the Hebrew faith, their Sheol, or Hades with its Gehenna and Paradise, they surely had a hope beyond the grave, and their traditions and the Apocrypha hold much of this precious faith. Surely there were sceptics, the mocking Sadducees. There are yet. No revelation has been made which demonstrates immortality. It is moral evidence which opens and burns to a thrilling hope in every willing mind. Even here it is especially true. "The path of the just shineth more and more unto the perfect day."

VIII

KNOWING THE DOCTRINE

"If any man will do His will, he shall know of the doctrine, whether it be of God, or whether I speak of myself."

JOHN vii. 17.

UPON everything God has touched He has put the traces of His fingers. Nothing which has emanated from Him is without some voice to speak of its Maker; nothing which is born is without some sign of its nativity. The minutest insect which floats in the air carries its credentials; the meanest shrub which grows bears on every leaf and blossom the divine patent, and every snow-flake or sunbeam comes sparkling in the light with the crystal seal of God.

So if God has come to us with a great system of salvation we may be sure it has come with "certain infallible proofs." And, beside its outer signals of prophecy and mighty works, and all this necessary paraphernalia of revelation, there will be something in its intrinsic nature which shows the finger of God. Will it not come with its impervious logic, with its white vestments of purity, and a face radiant with its own divinity, thrusting aside our doubts, and taking our hearts by the force of its own goodness?

So Christianity came, foretelling the future; came opening the eyes of the blind; raising the dead; casting out devils; saying to the sceptic, "Believe me for the very work's sake"; pointing to the page of history, whose events were mirrored in the vision of holy men of old; leading through the miraculous scenes of Judæa, and from the empty tomb to the fresh wounds of the risen Saviour, bidding him "Reach hither thy hand and be not faithless, but believing." But it came, too, with a more heavenly heraldry than even the miracles of Jesus, a voice more potent than the dead prophet, a "tongue of fire," teaching the conscience, and an abiding power to do greater things than the living Christ when He had gone to the Father.

It brought a system of truth able to speak for itself, so peerless, so sovereign, so supernal in its effect that the soul which looks aright must be smitten with a conviction of its origin. Jesus here invites the sceptic Jew, the sceptic world, to a test by which He professes the divinity of His doctrine shall be revealed: "If any man will do His will, he shall know of the doctrine, whether it be of God, or whether I speak of myself." The appeal to the external evidence is, "Go, walk about Zion, tell the towers thereof, mark ye well her bulwarks," but here, by this test, Jesus offers to take you by the hand, offers to lead you within the Holy City into the very sanctuary of God's Temple. And closeted in this pavilion of the Almighty, this secret place of the tabernacle of the Most High, what revelation of His truth, His love, His mercy, what an unveiling of His face, as we behold the beauty of the Lord, as we inquire in His Temple!

This condition is in harmony with the nature of mind. Be willing to do the will of God, to do as far as you know, and you shall be convinced; willing to walk as far as you see, and you shall see clearly. Willingness to do is the imperative condition of knowledge; it involves openness to conviction. Can you convince a man against his will? "None so blind as those who will not see," is the common-sense of the world carried into proverb. It is hard to prove the truth to one who is not willing to obey it; by any process of logic to force a conclusion home upon a man when it strikes his selfish life. He may not be able to detect any fallacy in the argument, conscience begins to stir and a voice from the soul says it must be true, but another force rises up and smothers the truth, saying, "It cannot be, there is some mistake; it touches my business, my habits, my happiness, if it is so." So the Jews could not find any fault in Jesus, in His life, His speech, or His doctrine —that trinity of evidence—but they were not convinced; and He said, "This is the condemnation that light has come into the world and men love darkness rather than light." One may be honest in his doubts and think he is in search for the truth, but if he is unwilling to follow as he finds it, he is really prejudiced against it. He does not, cannot, give the truth a fair chance. He unconsciously shrinks from the light which begins to shine upon a path in which he does not wish to walk. Sin wraps the soul in its evil desires and submerges it in a flood of passion like an ironclad in the ocean, invincible against all the batteries of heaven. The doubt of a single sin hugged to the heart is mail enough to run all the blockades of revelation. The fault is not in the evidence, the light shineth in utter darkness. The geologist will stand in his lecture-room and take you in thought to some river gorge where the stream has worn its bed down through the soil and solid rock, through strata of rocks, and back upon its course, and from its progress in a given period will boldly figure up the years or ages since that river began to run; he will take you back to chaos and build the world for you and shape the continents, mould the mountains, scoop out the seas, and cut the course of rivers by the power of his logic. It is easy to win your faith even on such probabilities. The astronomer will tell you he has seen a hazy something like a vapory cloud about that distant planet, that he thinks there are clouds like those in our sky, and, if so, an atmosphere; and, if so, life, and if life it is probably swarming with beings like these which people this earth, and if that planet, the next, and so on through the realms of God. You believe it because it is scientific, and the universe seems warmer and more sociable because so thickly settled; believe it because there is nothing in all this reasoning which makes a draft upon the exchequer or the conscience. The stars will shine on all the same and ask no favors of us; they will not go into an eclipse if we believe a false science; old mother earth will not stop rolling and swallow us up; she will not shut up her bowels of compassion even if we cherish a false geology. But men are conscious that this doctrine of Jesus means something. Like the baptism of John, if they admit it is from heaven they must receive it, if they admit the logic which proves it divine they must admit its divine sequence, which is the sum of all Christian duty; and if it says "Thou shalt love God," and "thou shalt love thy neighbor," the doctrine is a system of salvation which is "one and inseparable." Above, within it, burns a world of blessedness beyond thought; beneath it burns a world of woe just as eternal; and between them is the cross upon which is written in blood, "That whosoever believeth in Him should not perish, but have everlasting life;" and if one admits it is of God it brings a crisis upon his selfish soul. Hence it is hard to convince one if he is not willing to obey. You might argue until doomsday and his blind soul

will not see a flash of daylight. But let him be willing
to do the right as far as he sees the right, take off the
bandages of sin, pull back the bolts, and fling open the
shutters, and a whole hemisphere of sun will come in
and roll back the stone from the sepulchre, and the
soul, like dead Lazarus, will leap and fly intuitively
toward the truth. The soul is native in the truth and
turns to it as a flower to the sun. It welcomes the light,
drinks it in until in its quivering pulse and glowing
beauty it owns the sovereign Source. When one thus
opens to conviction by only resolving to obey the truth,
how fast the evidence comes flashing in; every word
sparkles, every promise seems full and thrilling, every
prayer breathes of heaven, until he is astonished at his
own doubts. Sometimes it is as vivid as if he had heard
the very voice of Jesus, and the light of Damascus had
shone again.

Perhaps it was because, in his blind zeal, Saul of
Tarsus thought he was doing the will of God that this
glorious vision burst from the skies. It came that he
"might know of the doctrine." God will not let a sin-
cere soul go long in the dark. If he begins in some
path of duty he will find the burning bush. A man can
hold up a prism so that it will grow dark in a sunbeam.
But now he begins to see the truth at the right angle,
through the lens of a willing heart, and every precept
and promise, every thought and argument becomes illu-

minated, and the whole doctrine of Christ towers in its real majesty. We have but to see the doctrine in its intrinsic beauty, as it is, to feel its birthright, even as a star flings out the burning sign of its Maker and rides on in the heavens. As we look we seem to hear its song, "The hand that made me is divine."

This spirit of obedience is the genius of all knowledge, for this willingness to do goes into practice; puts the theory to actual test to prove its divinity. Such a one reads the Golden Rule and tries it and feels its holy charm among the passions of men. He finds the law of mercy, of benevolence, and, like the Samaritan, tries it on his suffering neighbor and feels the overflowing benediction of his God measured into his glad soul. He hears of self-denial and repentance, and he breaks off his sins by righteousness and turns to God and takes up the cross. He hears the doctrine of forgiveness, of peace with God through our Lord Jesus Christ, and a voice, "He that believeth on the Son hath life." With honest soul, upon his knees, he puts it to the test and there fulfils the word of the Son of God, "he shall know of the doctrine"; he feels upon his sad soul as the kiss of God the seal of its dignity.

Jesus stakes the authority of the mission for which He dared to die and all His claims as the Messiah upon this test. Let a man try the experiment and see if there will not ultimately come an assurance sweet and strong as the song which broke upon the shepherds. He will start in darkness and gloom, and the first truth he tests will feel like a two-edged sword in his shrinking soul, piercing his dark thoughts and starting the crimson drops of sorrow. And yet in the very shadow which greets him, which is the shadow of his sins, there is a dim sense of the divine; he has entered an experience, a spiritual realm, in which the truth and even the facts of revelation seem to be re-enacted. In his own conscience he feels the power of the law, as if the old flaming, thundering mountain of the desert were in his shaking heart and the heavens above black as midnight, until in his gloom a star like that of Bethlehem arrives and the blush of a new morning is on the sky. Then again, in some way of duty, he goes on beneath his cross until he emerges from the mist into the clear sunlight of heaven; again he grasps some deeper fact of this system, goes higher, puts another truth in his wing of faith and continues his eagle flight above all clouds, and visions like those of Patmos are floating in his soul. The spirit of obedience thus leads to faith and faith to the very throne of God.

This is the scientific test for which the world is clamoring, and it is the only route to perfect assurance. The student in the school-room may master the text-book of chemistry, know the signs of every element and substance and repeat the formulas, but he must go into the laboratory and put his theory through the retort of the chemist and test these formulas before he has a reasonable trust in the science. So he may test these formulas of grace in prayer and fiery trials, and let him find one in this great text-book of salvation which is a failure. There is a latent force in these promises which, when the conditions are fulfilled, is liberated and proves to be the power of God unto salvation.

The workmen who began to work out the design of Angelo in the grand structure of St. Peter's must have had at the start but dim shadowy thoughts of the great temple, and many an apprentice probably shook his head at the result of such a unique style of architecture and such vast proportions; but as year after year they toiled under the tuition of that master spirit they saw the beauty of the unfolding plan until at last as they walked beneath its massive arches and looked up into the mighty dome next to heaven and felt its grandeur they must have bowed before that genius and the divinity of his design.

So if one stops in the theory of Christianity and asks to be convinced, to see the whole design, even an angel cannot dissolve the mysteries; and as he stays the more shadowy his thoughts until they fade into empty doubt; but let him start and put the faith he has into solid work, or breathe it out in prayer, and it will crystallize into holy character and into forms of living beauty.

Thus one willing to work out the plan of the Master under the tuition of the Spirit shall at length walk with joy beneath the arched mysteries of redemption and gaze into the infinite dome of the Trinity with triumphant faith.

Hume's argument against the possibility of proving a miracle rests in this: That we have never witnessed such a sign of divine power; we did not stand upon that river bank and see the tide rolled backward to let His people pass; we did not see Jesus stilling the storm; did not stand by the sea when Jesus put His feet upon the buoyant waves and walked to the other shore. No one living has ever seen a miracle; we have no experience in miracles. And so he puts our experience, or rather want of experience, against the testimony of those who lived in the days of revelation. But here is a living miracle which will last as long as time, and which any man may experience if he will do His will, however little his faith; a miracle wrought in the soul, as real as the resurrection of Lazarus or the transfiguration of Christ; in which a dead soul is raised into a new life whose horizon is eternity and in which a dark nature is transfigured into the image of God. Thus can we "know of the doctrine." This is the everlasting sign of Jesus.

So if we have taken any section of this arch and proved it perfect, divine, is not the whole great circle perfect, true, beautiful as the form we see? We may thus be conscious of all God's doctrine.

An illustration of this is found in Dr. Liefchild's story of an interview with a poor lad he met among the mountains of Ireland.

"Can you read?" I asked.

"To be sure I can."

"And do you understand what you read?"

"A little."

"Let us hear you," and I turned his attention to the third chapter of the Gospel of John, which he seemed readily to find, and said, "Now read." He did so with a clear, unembarrassed voice:

" 'There was a man of the Pharisees, named Nicodemus, a ruler of the Jews: the same came to Jesus by night, and said unto him, Rabbi.' "

"What does that mean?"

"It means master. 'We know that thou art a teacher come from God: for no man can do these miracles that thou doest, except God be with him.' "

"What is a miracle?"

"It is a great wonder. 'Jesus answered and said unto him, Verily, verily, I say unto thee.' "

"What does 'verily' signify?"

"It means 'indeed.' 'Except a man be born again.' "

"What is that?"

"It means," he promptly replied, "a great change.

'Except a man be born again, he cannot see the kingdom of God.' "

"And what is that kingdom?"

He paused, and with an expression of seriousness and devotion which I never shall forget, placing his hand upon his bosom, he said, "It is something here"; and then raising his eyes, he added, "and something up yonder."

If we are conscious of a "kingdom in here," we know there is a kingdom yonder, mansions in the Father's house.

Then, it follows from the very nature of this divine knowledge that God will not, perhaps cannot, thrust it upon us any more than any other knowledge; it must be won like science, beginning at the alphabet, willing to do as far as we know. Who dreams of calculus and astronomy who will not learn arithmetic? And yet men want to know all this deepest doctrine of the universe before they will spell the first syllable in prayer; before they will bend a knee. They want a demonstration of the being of God or the Trinity, a solution of the problem of sin and an analysis of redemption, and all these doctrines clustering around the cross which can only be seen from the cross in salvation. Some start, and because at the first resolve, the first tear, they do not have a revelation like that of St. Paul's in paradise, they turn back. They must go on just as when a man stumbles on in the rain and mist. He walks as far as he sees, and, as he advances, the mist rises at every step until he comes out of the valley, out of the mist into the beautiful world filled with all its wondrous displays of God's power and glory. So may they come up from the cold shadow of death into immortality, leaving the black floods of Jordan rolling below.

And then the converse is just as true: If any man will not do His will he shall not know of the doctrine. Here is the cause of weakness, of doubt, of dreaming, and despair. Though he may have "climbed where Moses stood," the instant he shrank from duty, shrank from the path where the light shone, that instant a film gathered over his eye, the horizon grew dim, and the farther he went the deeper the darkness, until the doctrine was a web of mist and God a phantom of the soul.

When that voice came to Abraham, commanding him to go and offer up his only son, I have wondered if he did not question that revelation and if, in that three days' journey to Moriah, doubts did not haunt him. But this I know, that, doubting or believing, he went on in the way waiting for the unfolding, and, at the last, as he bound his darling son on the altar and lifted the gleaming knife above his throat, the solution came. It is this spirit of obedience that is the key which unlocks the successive revelations of the Spirit. From light to light, from star to star, from glory to glory, forever.

The path of duty may start in tears and lead through shadows and along that rugged mountain pass where sweeps the tempest, but the vultures of doubt do not hover over it. The "Angel of His presence" at the end of every stage is a Beulah and the last stage is heaven.

IX

ABRAM WATCHING THE SACRIFICE

"And when the fowls came down upon the carcases, Abram drove them away."

GENESIS XV. 11.

IT is night in Hebron. We see an old man, nearly a century old, standing by his tent; over him bends the brilliant Oriental sky; his face is upward; he is rapt by the gorgeous picture; the night winds are playing with his white locks. Great emotions stir his soul. It is the man of Chaldea in communion, not with the stars, but with the God who made them. He has just heard in his tent the same awful voice which called him out of Ur, bidding him go out and count the stars as the signs of his posterity. He sees in them the faces of millions who shall look back to him. No king or conqueror in his wildest ambition ever had such a vision.

Abram believes God. He then and there takes into his heart God's mighty promise lettered in stars, "and it was counted to him for righteousness." Then and there, by his lone tent, too, he receives the right and title to his vast estate in the "Land of promise." And to ratify this contract God appoints the usual sign. Abraham takes the sacrifices and divides them in the midst and lays each piece one against another, for contracting parties were wont to pass between the parted limbs of the slain animals with an imprecation that in case of a breach in the treaty it might be done to them as to the animals.

So Abram passes between them and waits for God to ratify the contract, the "Old Testament." All through that long day he waits. The sun rises higher in the heavens, its mid-day beams pour down on the slain victims, and still there is no coming of God.

The birds of prey scent the blood and come flying to the place; they are fierce and ravening, but Abram drives them back and stands guard by the sacrifice, lest it be polluted and devoured. The sun is going down, and wearied by his long vigil he sinks into a deep sleep. In that sleep comes a prophetic vision. A horror of darkness falls upon him, which he is told symbolizes four hundred years of slavery for his people, out of which they shall come back to home and freedom. He awakes, and again it is night, and as he looks toward the sacrifice, lo, a smoking furnace and a burning lamp pass between those pieces. The flesh changes into the sweet savor of sacrifice floating away to heaven. The fiery seal of Jehovah is affixed to the deed of conveyance, and Abram knows by divine right that he stands on his own soil. Through all that weary day God kept Abram waiting and watching; waiting for His coming and watching the sacrifice. But without flinching or fretting that grand old man waited the Lord's motion; the burning symbol of His presence then walked between the bleeding limbs, and, at last, when the patriarch slept in death, that vision was marvellously verified in the rolling years.

Now prove to me, if you can, that there was no Abraham, and no such transaction; impeach the story and make it a myth, yet every Christian man would know that the author of the grand parable, if it is one, drew the picture to the life. Just that historic scene of Hebron comes to pass in the life of every man who comes to God in any dispensation. That religious drama, though without bleeding limbs and real fire, is vividly carried out in every experience. Its principle lies deep in our nature and in the nature of God. The voice of God! A call! Down in the conscience it echoes; above him bend the same heavens, set full of God's promises! And, acting from his faith in Him "Who cannot lie," faith in His abounding grace through the great atonement, he, like Abram, brings and lays before God, in utter submission, his offering for the consummation of the treaty. The offering evinces his faith and submission and sincerity. The essential idea is man giving himself over to God and God giving Himself over to man.

The man is not saved on account of this self-offering, but solely on account of God's mercy, offered through the great sacrifice. It is not in its nature a bargain, as if a sinner should say, "O God, if Thou wilt pardon my sins and give me eternal life, I will give Thee myself." Not that, for already, by every possible right, he belongs to God, and has been defrauding Him of His own in every year of sin. But in answer to God's overture of life and pardon, he simply accepts His terms. God forgives because of His own pure mercy. He is able to forgive and be just through His own great sacrifice. He actually does forgive when the man penitently submits at His feet and accepts His mercy, and that is faith—showing that he accepts by offering himself to God in harmony with the great transaction.

It is more the nature of the marriage contract. The great Creator comes a-wooing. He offers Himself in His ineffable beauty and grandeur, in all His unutterable blessedness and being, to the creature. Out of the love of His great heart He sues for acceptance. He points to His mansion and waits as a lover, "Give Me thine heart"; and any acceptance implies that giving, even though not the meritorious reason of salvation. Then the sweet sign of that grand treaty, the burning kiss of betrothal, will come to the soul consenting to the divine union with its Infinite lover, as it sings with a bride's light in the eye, "'Tis done, the great transaction's done. I am my Lord's and He is mine."

Hence you see that this offering is at the basis of any

treaty with God. In its very nature it must be supposed at the initial and at every stage of the Christian life. The withholding of self from God is the very heart of sin, and there cannot be a genuine tear of godly sorrow or a single act of faith without this coming back. What has God of a man if He has not his heart? The crouching obeisance of a slave; the bloodless forms of a legal contract; the stretching out of cold jeweled fingers in the ceremony of a forced marriage. It is a corpse on the altar before God, and never yet on such an offering fell a spark of fire out of heaven.

We sometimes hear of "entire consecration"—as if any other sort will do in this contract. Consecration is the bowing of the man, the supreme self to the Supreme love, the great "I" to the great "I AM." You can see at a glance that it lies in the will, the purpose, the motive, and if the will yields all but a little it does not yield at all. A resolve to be right in all but a little is a resolve not to be right. A conscious keeping back at all is conscious insincerity, and the Eye which looks down the soul to the bottom sees it, the offering, a cheat, a sham, which is the very essence of the crime of Ananias and Sapphira. In this solemn treaty it can get no sign but that which smote that guilty pair at the apostle's feet as an awful warning for the church.

At the very start of seeking God there must be sincerity or entire consecration in purpose, or that pious fraud will recoil in the blight of unbelief, more terrible in the end than that silent stroke which blanched in death the cheeks of those old perjurers. Just so is it essential in all subsequent dealings with God. To enter into the full possession of the estate of God there must be this solid basis of honor in the absolute and unconditional devotion to Him; in new tests, in some crisis of experience, some lifting of the eyes to His stars in the heaven of His love. In every step up among His stars, like Abram, we must stand by our offering looking into the promises. It was the same start with Enoch. The very word Enoch means devoted. It was the name of a man who "walked with God" so closely that Heaven set in before the frosts of death could strike him.

In the first seeking of God, however, to test this sincerity, to draw out the soul in desire, and so in larger faith, God often, though not always, keeps us waiting. All day until the going down of the sun, Abram stood by his sacrifice. So, often, from the calling of God beneath the stars, all during the night of conviction, even by his offering, the sad smitten man may wait for the witness of pardon. Or, in the deeper throes for some special grace or in some great trial, we may be kept waiting as we sing, "My all is on the altar." In that waiting comes the danger. There is the fatal spot where many fail just on the eve of great success; at the very break of day, the threshold of this crystal palace of life and rest, when the porter's hand is on the latch, just at this time in the tide of your great affairs, when the flood is come to lead you on to life and everlasting fortune; just when you feel that you have obeyed, you have counted the cost, you have accepted the overtures of heaven through the Redeemer and presented yourself, saying, "Here, Lord." How long it seems you have stood waiting! But see yonder, through the evening sky the witness of a covenant-keeping God is just breaking. There is hovering over the offering an ill-omened bird, a bird of prey. Its ghostly form is thin as thought. You may not discern it unless your eye is keen. It is swift of wing as the falcon and its beak and talons fierce and fatal to the offering. Its name is Doubt. "Perhaps it was not God's voice I heard. It may be I have not sought aright or sorrowed deep and long enough for sin. Who knows about this change? What a mystery! Perhaps God does not answer prayer. Even some good men think that prayer does not move God. Maybe I am passed by and left out like poor Esau, and there is no mercy at all for me." And then another bird, black as the raven, called Despair, settles down on the offering. And no offering, no life is safe, however long it has been on the altar or how often the fiery witness has walked over the soul. This is the day of doubt. It is in the air. This vulture flies in books and pamphlets and newspapers, into our doors and windows. Its feathers shine with gilt and gold. The fire of genius flashes from its eyes. It croaks of science and caves and tombs where it lives, and boasts of flights among the stars. But it is rank of the dead where it has revelled. Its flapping puts out the light of joy in the home, the light of life from the soul. Its ruthless talons tear human hearts from the altar of God. You cannot read doubt or think doubt, much less let it brood on the soul night and day, without harm. If you believe that it is necessary for you to study it to meet by the truth its arguments and fallacies for the sake of others, still it is dangerous. Perhaps not to your orthodoxy. You may have mental acumen and skill to refute the error and stand firm in the "faith once delivered to the saints"; you may be able to rout and scout the error as you hear or read, but even then you cannot keep your thoughts forever playing with these fiery darts of the devil without feeling a blight on the soul. You can't keep company with these ghosts without being haunted. Suppose you sit down in a dark room, in a *séance* of spiritualists, ever so bold in your own belief that it is an occult science or a fraud, yet you may feel a chill creeping on you as if spirit hands were feeling you. And so here, as you see that sneer on the lip of that lecturer whose wit fascinates, or you read it in your literary magazine or charming novel, only a sneer at Christ or prayer; it is not argument, it is usually used for want of argument; it is a cheap way of knifing the hated truth, like the wagging of heads at the Saviour. You know it is nothing, but you can't answer it and it haunts you; your logic goes through it like the fist of a drunkard through the phantoms of delirium and leaves the same gibing face and leer. There are souls whose very closets are frescoed with such "shapes of Tartarus"; people who praise the Bible, are sure its truths are precious, that they come down from heaven, and they are to light lost souls through this night of sin up the white stairs of life, but those souls are by day and often by night feeding on sneers coined in the hearts of atheists.

Another group of birds is likely to be there wherever they see or scent a sacrifice. It is slow of wing and foot and does not swoop down on the prey like the eagle. It creeps up and is sly and insidious. But it is just as rapacious and deadly. A spirit of impatience and fretfulness, which is fatal, often comes over a man in this waiting. It seems to him he has done everything in his power, done enough. He has given himself to God; renounced every sinful thing and, full of godly sorrow for his sins, has thrown himself on his Saviour; and yet the hours go by and no answer. Just here this black spirit drops on him and he cries, "It is no use; I can't get hold of it; it's a hard thing, this religion"; and he flashes fire, gives up, turns on his heel from the altar, and there he is, out in the world, harder than common sinners. That spirit of impatience is not the spirit of sacrifice.

This vulture tears away the whole offering at one fell swoop. In this treaty you had made over yourself as an offering to God. The element of time was not in it. It was His own. You had no more to do with it, no right to take it back. Your part was now just to wait for His salvation and watch the offering against these birds of prey.

Or possibly in that crisis there creeps on to the offering this other bird, which has the motion of the sloth, the cunning and heart of the serpent. The eye grows dull, the eager, upturned face loses its light; the keen zest and desire for the salvation of God dies out of the soul. Slothfulness! Spiritual laziness! How many come to this point and "count the cost," and for a moment "count all things but loss." They are in earnest. They hunger and thirst. They look toward the cross. But the service closes, the sermon is over, or the revival, and so is their seeking. They give up until next time, and then every time fall short. They relapse into indifference and indolence. They become religiously shiftless; not enough in earnest to read the Bible or pray in secret, and largely forget the means of grace. These half-hearted seekers of religion and half-hearted professors seeking more grace and a higher life knock at other doors until their hands are black with bruises. They writhe in thought and heart and knot their muscles in the arena of life. They wait in the white heat of supplication at the feet of the goddess of the world to catch a smile from her fickle lips; but with the breath of a frozen heart they come to God and whisper, "Lord, Lord," for forgiveness of sin, the gift of the Holy Ghost, and eternal salvation, and give up before the swiftest angel could reach them. God cannot bless such heartlessness. They sink down by their altar asleep. This bird of ill-omen has spread its soft feathers over the soul and a death-like stupor has crept all through it. But perchance the soul may sleep until "the horror of darkness" will come on and prophetic visions of more than Egypt's bondage.

Then there is another, which wears the plumage of the bird of paradise. Men call it Pleasure. It has no talons, but beneath its deceitful song and hovering the sacrifice melts away as if smitten by the lightnings. I need not tell that soul once anxiously seeking, feeling after God, or once happy in the joys of His love and full of the Christian's hope, how deep is the sleep which has fallen.

Once more, it is the winged monster of the myth, "having the face of a woman and the body of a vulture, with long claws and with a face pale with hunger." It is the harpy of evil habit; it is no myth; the lusts which through long years of indulgence have grown into habit; how they all gather about a man when he is trying to be good, when he is seeking God, and often after years of Christian living, when waiting before Him for a blessing, how suddenly they will swoop down on him, when he thinks they are dead. These harpies are fierce, and persistent, and hard-lived.

Then the cares of life, anxieties, whole flocks of little winged things, hover over and vex and annoy and steal away the sacrifice; and doubtless more men are hindered and blighted by these flocks of sparrows and swarms of gnats than by the great birds of prey; more are cheated out of great blessings and great happiness, if not out of heaven, by these little harpies of life.

But watching our sacrifice, beating back the birds of prey, we develop a patient earnestness and a faith which can cling to the promise of God until, like Abraham, the flesh wilts in weariness by the sacrifice and all other light goes down. And then will He wake us to see a revelation of Himself brighter than that which burned on the altar of Mamre.

X

OUR RESPONSIBILITIES TO THE TWENTIETH CENTURY

ALL the way here for a fifteen minutes' paper on Responsibilities to the Twentieth Century! That is, for nineteen centuries gone! Fifteen minutes for nineteen centuries! Well, it is so bewildering; fifteen minutes are about as good as fifteen hours!

I did not come on foot or on a bicycle. I rode on a steam-car—velvet cushions, spring seats, iron track, and drawn by a great live engine—and was only thirty minutes coming. Of course I paid my fare, full fare, and yet, for the fine style of this expedition in this twentieth-century chariot, I suppose something extra is due to somebody; but Stephenson is dead and Watt is dead, and the mechanics, for aught I know; and the conductor and engineer are paid by the company, and I don't propose to pay Mr. Carnegie a royalty on my ride. So, then, to whom is my extra responsibility? I must be in debt to somebody.

Now, just as you can show up the amount of the value of this style of conveyance over the old stage-coach, I suppose you have a clear case against me, and I might as well confess judgment and let it go upon record as a lien on my personal effects! Then, too, if you can present a like bill for superior illuminations, gas, electricity, education, facilities for knowledge, livelihood and happiness, for a better house, better clothes, better food—if not more of it—you may so load me down with hopeless indebtedness that I might as well make a general assignment. And to whom? All the old worthies are dead. They have gone beyond our poor recompense. Then our debt of obligation must be due to this and the coming generation, and our devotion to Him who owns all, and Whose we are, and Whom we serve, if we are Christians.

Now we may fall in with the seeming tendency of society to depreciate the higher things of our civilization, but, after all, men unconsciously confess their value, while from their commonness they often ignore and, maybe, despise.

Our millions of material inventions of which we boast came because they were wanted. The people wanted a better conveyance than the canal-boat and stage, so Stephenson and Fulton got up the locomotive and the steamer. They wanted a better light than the tallow dip, and Edison stuck up our electric stars. There were too many people in the world to be dressed by the old wheel and homespun, so Arkwright thought of the spinning jenny. The old hand needle was too slow, and

OUR RESPONSIBILITIES

Elias Howe filled the world with the hum of the sewing-machine. The whisperers wanted a wider neighborhood, and Bell made the telephone. They wanted to kill by wholesale, and they traded the tomahawk for the shrapnel. If the world did not want these things it would put them out of the back door with the rubbish. It won't blow out its arc lights, pull down its telegraphs, and cashier its inventions. They are the occasion of trouble. They make hard times for many an old-fashioned mechanic. They get up trusts. They crowd people into the cities in masses of suffering and vice. Who can tell all the mischief incident to these growing products of the human brain, which, at the same time, men idolize as if they were the very glory of the age and the elements of a physical paradise.

Why, then, if not wanted, do they sustain these other institutions? Why support this burden of the Bible? Cashier the clergy; fire the churches; raze the colleges of our Christian education; shut down this ado about religion; quit this hue about the soul and eternal life; stop the mouth of prayer; put out this hope and fear; put out Heaven; put out God! Fence up this haunted field called the Kingdom of Heaven, and post up your proscriptions, "No more digging in this field for hid treasures." Of course, the world would do this if it could; if it felt it could get along without it and be comfortable! If it could, it would cut its throat and go to pieces in French revolutions.

The church makes plenty of trouble—occasions bloody wars—some say the missionaries have made the fuss in China. Then it costs a great deal. Religion is an expensive luxury. Why not do without it? Many do. Go tell it to-morrow from house to house, at the door of the mansion, the cottage of the poor; tell it to the tempted, the mourner, shout it over the cemetery, chisel it off the tombs—Religion an outcast! Nay, you gloomy iconoclast, go on to the finish, vote it out of your soul and conscience. The mighty speculation would soon come to grief if you could spoil the market. But as your motherless children would cry in your empty house if that mother's life went out to-night, so would your orphan soul cry after its lost God. And the world itself would not sleep nights for fear its treasures might be stolen and it might die before morning! And so, even unchristian people had rather share the responsibilities of our Christianity, its churches, its education, its colleges, its asylums, its missions, its hope!

Then, too, we are responsible for the best grade and type of all products of this Christian life and age, and so for a trained and consecrated mind. For this we must sharpen the instincts of industry. It is not a lucky find, not often. The law of gravitation was not an evolution of the apple. Columbus did not blunder on the new

world. Paradise Lost was not an apocalypse. The Greek
Slave was not a discovery. The cotton-gin did not grow
on the bushes. It is all by the cunning of men whose wits
have grown keen in inquiry. The merchant-man sought
the pearls. The pearls have an affinity for such pains.
They love to be found by such hunters. They take to the
bosoms of those who covet their charms, but shrink from
the cold heart of stupidity. God doesn't put His jewels
in your raid for common stuff; He does not scatter them
in the highway. Swine are good diggers, but they do not
care for pearls. Only elect souls which have grown great
in honest discipline and prayer get Ezekiel's vision of
God's beauty or find the Holy Grail.

There is very much more in all realms to be learned
to-day, and we get no better start. A baby knows no
more, not even a Twentieth Century baby. True, the
outlines have been surveyed, the pioneers are long since
at rest, but in one great sense every one is a pioneer.
Each must discover the old things over again, solve the
problems, start at the beginning, and it is not easy to
walk in the steps of those old giants. And then, it is a
bad heresy to assert that there is nothing new. There
are skies overhead in every domain, anxious, as God's
other promises, to show their secrets. There are steps
of which Jacob's Ladder was but a shadow, and there
are no favorites but those who climb, no limits but the

gravity of our own minds. We can go through soon as any angel when our wings are grown.

Often the croakers cry "Nothing new," when their feet are only wet in the puddle of their own conceit close by the ocean. Fulton's boat was new, was it not? Morse's telegraph? The Iliad? Macbeth? Ericsson's Monitor? There are many new things ahead—inventions, books, poems, sermons, some better, and some perhaps worse. True, the steam and iron were old; the iron and glass of Herschel's telescope, the acid and zinc of Volta's battery, the charcoal of Edison's light, also the colors of Angelo's frescos, the notes of Haydn's oratorio; gravity and nature old, yet all these new as if fresh miracles of God. "Nothing new" is a calumny on the Creator. His mines are not all worked; His wells are not pumped dry; His music not all sung; His riddles not all guessed. He has enough to keep eternity green, and yonder on the glowing skies we may yet see "His ways are past finding out."

No one who has had a taste of honest work and divine teaching will be content with the old routine in nature or grace any more than Moses in his desert, after he had seen the burning bush. Such a mind will get up an exodus. It may pass over the old routes, but the places where the great seers have walked will never be barren; it may pitch its tent in the same old desert, but will make it an Elim and drink out of the rock, and find pasturage in the teeming heavens.

This is the responsibility to-day: to go down into the old rocks of geology, the old laboratories of the chemist, into the shops of the mechanic, into old languages, old documents, for truer science, truer history, truer biology. Old skies, but new telescopes to see them deeper. The old Bible, but better exegesis to see it deeper. It does not need piecing out, but our minds need piecing out. The skies do not need piecing out, but our eyes. And God's Bible, no more than the Pleiades. "Nay, heaven and earth shall pass away, but the word of God shall stand forever."

Then there are more things we want to know more about. There are mysteries about the common things enough to keep the savants humble. What the nature of the atom? The number of essential elements? What of the existence and nature of ether, that mythical light-bearer which floats the sunlight over the abysses of space? How the earth got here if it did not slip off the sun, and the when and the how of it? Even how the mountains were made? The nature of life itself and the mysterious What after it?

And to be sure, we want nothing but the truth, and only he is a bigot who is not open to it all. It was said that a few years ago a lawyer came to this country from England and dug up and sifted the dust of three old graves to find a signet-ring, with which to identify the seals of an important document. We ought to be willing to have the testing of our most sacred things, though the mould of centuries is on them, if any signets can be found which can identify the truth, no matter whose hope is blasted or whose opinions fit the seal. But we want honest sextons and competent sifters. We cannot trust the analysis of ghouls. We do not want our infinite interests tampered with by jugglers. There are smart pagans who are paid for manipulating the most momentous things of this world and the next, and who cheat the sincerest brains with proved scientific jugglery. They exert a mesmeric sway over faith and character. They profess to be piously searching for the truth. They say they are sifting the creeds and sacred records, but they are sifting with daggers. So we are responsible for trained minds which can expose fraud, sift all things and "hold fast that which is good." And for this there must be Christian schools and universities.

Then, in order to reach and sustain the best fashions of an age, in the material, intellectual and spiritual, we have to consider one more "'bility," our financial responsibility. Yes, it costs something to be a Christian, but Christ says it pays more than it costs. If the Christian world should suddenly shut down on its benevolence what a paralysis, swift as the lightning, would strike the earth like the Day of Doom! Who could send the telegrams? It would be a smaller surprise to read in leaders to-morrow, "The springs of the Great Lakes failed and Niagara River dried up! Only a little stream trickles over the Falls!" Do you think there are any fires which can dry up this river of love, whose springs are yonder on the slopes of Olivet?

It seems a piece of audacity for the Boards to appropriate millions to the needs of our work and not a dollar in sight. Then for our Bishops to talk of an extra twenty millions after that awful cry which has filled the world with its more dismal echoes, that we have lost a few of our members out of the millions. We ought to lose some more; we would be vastly stronger as a church. But our gifts are on their way to the treasury of Christ's poor in solid rivers of gold, and our drafts are good for their face in all the money markets of the globe.

Now perhaps God might have made each man to exist alone. Eliminate sympathy and love, and after this how much of a man have you left? What a poor, stingy scrap of God's image! Such a man would hardly be worth saving anyway, and no matter who gets the job. God might have set up the world as a great boarding-house, and raised us in a crystal palace, like the fish in the sea, and made us cold-blooded as a fish for his fellows, but He did not. He made us like Himself, and we must stand up in a man's place and take his burdens and his heritage. No man can shirk himself and be a fish if he wants to, though he may get very cold and hard to his brother; he, like a big fish, may eat up the little ones and wipe his mouth and say it is "according to the survival of the fittest." And so, to charm off the curses of avarice and keep the mildews from your roofs, you ought to chide your preacher, if he forgets to echo Christ's voice, which often seems like the boom of the billows from over the ocean, plaintive as the moan of the dying, and deep as the thunders of the last Judgment, "Inasmuch as ye did it not to one of the least of these, ye did it not to Me."

Are there not many who would find light on a hidden way? Would not the dark cloud which hovers over them break in splendors, as if rent by an angel's hand, and let through the glory, if only their hearts would open and entertain some other mercy on the earth?

I believe there are many barren souls in the church, whose wrestling prayers wring very little moisture out of the brooding heavens, because they have so few tears for misery here; they may knock at the door with their petitions until they bleed and fall back dying, and not a smile can squeeze through a crevice on their lifted faces, if they bolt their hearts against the cries of our humanity, with its great, hungry eyes, like other prayers, and its bony hands stretched out for the crumbs under the table. And would not some of our great loaves, and luxuries, be sweeter and have more nourishment if we gave the crumbs or tithed them for the poor?

OUR RESPONSIBILITIES

God's promises are dry wells, over which the windlass creaks and rattles, and about which men with dry throats huddle and twist at the crank, and look with watery eyes into empty buckets, on which even the moss is dried, but "he that watereth shall be watered also himself."

Oh, when God's money is fretting in the pocket or bank-vault, when His smuggled tithes and offerings have been groaning like imprisoned angels, it is a disastrous swindle against our own souls if we expect any favors of heaven. The real spirit of piety is born out of that Bosom which carries the world, and which gets its richest revenues out of its costliest sacrifices. If so, our two millions, and twenty millions, would be poor, stingy apportionments for our Twentieth Century offering.

THE END